Hogarth ⓗ Shakespeare

NEW BOY

TRACY CHEVALIER

Hogarth Shakespeare
LONDON • NEW YORK

Published in the United States by Hogarth, an imprint of the Crown Publishing Group, a division of Penguin Random House LLC, New York.
www.crownpublishing.com

HOGARTH is a trademark of the Random House Group Limited, and the H colophon is a trademark of Random House LLC.

Simultaneously published in Great Britain by Hogarth UK, a division of Random House Group Limited, a Penguin Random House Company, London.

"Killing Me Softly," words and music by Charles Fox and Norman Gimbel © 1972 Rodali Music (BMI). All rights on behalf of Warner-Tamerlane Publishing Corp. and Rodali Music administered by Warner/Chappell North America Ltd. By permission of Imagem Music, an Imagem company.

Library of Congress Cataloging-in-Publication Data is available upon request.

ISBN 978-0-553-44763-7
Ebook ISBN 978-0-553-44764-4

Printed in the United States of America

Jacket design: Christopher Brand
Jacket illustration: Joni Majer

10 9 8 7 6 5 4 3 2 1

First United States Edition

PART I

BEFORE SCHOOL

Ice cream soda, cherry on top
Tell me the name of your sweetheart!

Dee noticed him before anyone else. She was glad of that, held on to it. It made her feel special to have him to herself for a few seconds, before the world around them skipped a beat and did not recover for the rest of the day.

The playground was busy before school. Enough children had arrived early that games of jacks and kickball and hopscotch had begun, to be abandoned when the bell rang. Dee herself had not been early—her mother had sent her upstairs to change her top for something looser, saying Dee had spilled egg on it, though Dee herself couldn't see any yolk. She'd had to run part of the way to school, braids thumping against her back, until the stream of students heading the same direction reassured her she was not late. She had gotten to the playground with a minute to spare before the first bell rang.

There hadn't been enough time to join her best friend, Mimi, jumping Double Dutch with the other girls, so instead Dee had headed to the playground entrance into the building, where Mr. Brabant was standing with other teachers, waiting for the class lines to form. Her teacher had a short, angled haircut that squared his head, and stood very straight. Someone told Dee he had fought in Vietnam. Dee was not the top student in class—that prize went to prim Patty—but she liked to please Mr. Brabant when she could, enough to make him notice her, though she knew she was sometimes called a teacher's pet.

She took her place at the front of the line now, and looked around, her eyes on the Double-Dutch girls still jumping rope. Then she spotted him, a motionless presence by the merry-go-round. Four boys were spinning on it—Ian and Rod and two boys from fourth grade. They were going so fast that Dee was sure one of the teachers would stop them. Once a boy had been flung off and broken an arm. The two fourth graders looked scared, but could not control the merry-go-round, as Ian was expertly kicking the ground to keep up the speed.

The boy standing near the frenetic motion was not dressed like the other boys, casual in their jeans and T-shirts and sneakers. Instead he wore gray flared pants, a white short-sleeve shirt, and black shoes, like a uniform a private school student would wear. But it was his skin that stood out, its color reminding Dee of bears she'd seen at the zoo a few months before, on a school field trip. Though they were called black bears, their fur was actually deep brown, with a reddish tint at the tips. They had mostly slept, or sniffed at the pile of grubs the keeper had dumped in the pen for them. Only when Rod threw a stick at the animals to impress Dee did one of the bears react, baring its yellow teeth and growling so that the children shrieked and laughed. Dee had not joined in, though; she had frowned at Rod and turned away.

The new boy was not watching the merry-go-round, but studying the L-shaped building. It was a typical suburban elementary school, built eight years before, and looked like two red-brick shoeboxes unimaginatively shoved together. When Dee had started kindergarten it still had a new building smell to it. Now, though, it was like a dress she had worn many times, with its tears and stains and marks where the hem had been let down. She knew every classroom, every staircase, every handrail, every bathroom cubicle. She knew every foot of the playground too, as well as the younger students' playground on the other side of the building. Dee had fallen off the swings, torn her tights on the slide, gotten stuck at the top of the jungle gym when she became too scared to climb down. Once she had declared one half of the playground Girl Town, and she and Mimi and Blanca and Jennifer had chased away any boy who dared to cross the line. She had hidden with others around the corner near the gym entrance, where teachers on duty couldn't see them and they could try on lipstick and read comics and play spin the bottle. She had lived her life on the playground, laughed and cried and had crushes and formed friendships and made few enemies. It was her world, so familiar she took it for granted. In a month she would be leaving it for junior high.

Now someone new and different had entered the

territory, and this made Dee look at the space anew and suddenly find it shabby, and herself an alien in it. Like him.

He was moving now. Not like a bear, with its bulky, lumbering gait. More like a wolf, or—Dee tried to think of dark animals—a panther, scaled up from house cats. Whatever he was thinking—probably about being the new boy in a playground full of strangers the opposite color from him—he padded toward the school doors where the teachers waited with the unconscious assuredness of someone who knows how his body works. Dee felt her chest tighten. She drew in a breath.

"Well, well," Mr. Brabant remarked. "I think I hear drums."

Miss Lode, the other sixth grade teacher standing next to him, tittered. "Where did Mrs. Duke say he's from?"

"Guinea, I think. Or was it Nigeria? Africa, anyway."

"He's yours, isn't he? Better you than me." Miss Lode smoothed her skirt and touched her earrings, perhaps to make sure they were still there. It was a nervous habit she repeated often. She kept her appearance neat, except for her short blond hair that puffed out in a curly bob. Today she wore a lime green skirt, a yellow blouse, and green disks clipped to her ears. Her shoes were also green, with low square heels. Dee and her friends loved discussing Miss Lode's wardrobe. She was a young teacher, but her clothes were nothing like her students' pink and white T-shirts and bell-bottom jeans with flowers embroidered along the hems.

Mr. Brabant shrugged. "I don't foresee problems."

"No, of course not." Miss Lode kept her wide blue eyes fixed on her colleague as if not wanting to miss any morsel of wisdom that might help her become a better teacher. "Do you think we should—well, *say* something to the students about him? About—I don't know—about him being *different*? To encourage them to welcome him?"

Mr. Brabant snorted. "Take off your kid gloves, Diane. He doesn't need special treatment just because he's bl— a new boy."

"No, but— No. Of course." Miss Lode's eyes turned watery. Mimi had told Dee that once or twice her teacher actually cried in class. Behind her back her students called her Cry Baby Lody.

Mr. Brabant's eyes came to rest on Dee waiting in front of him, and he cleared his throat. "Dee, go and round up the other girls." He gestured at the Double-Dutch jumpers. "Tell them I'll take away the ropes if they keep on skipping after the first bell rings."

He was one of the few male teachers in the school, and though it shouldn't have mattered, to Dee it made him the kind of teacher you always obeyed, the teacher you impressed if you could—the way she felt about her own father, whom she wanted to please when he came home from work.

She hurried over to the girls jumping Double Dutch; they were using two thick ropes that made a satisfying thwack on the asphalt, and chanting as they turned. She hesitated a moment, for it was Blanca's go. She was by far the best Double-Dutcher in school, jumping so nimbly as the ropes came around that she could go for minutes without getting tripped up. The other girls preferred chants that would require Blanca to call someone else into the ropes or send herself out. Blanca of course liked to stay in, and this morning had managed to get them to chant:

> Ice cream soda, cherry on top
> Tell me the name of your sweetheart!
> Is it A, B, C, D . . .

If the jumper didn't get caught on one of the letters, they went on to numbers up to twenty, then favorite colors. Blanca was going through the colors now, long black curls bouncing, feet nimble even though she was wearing platform sandals. Dee could never jump in such shoes; she preferred her white Converse sneakers, which she kept as clean as she could.

She went over to Mimi, who was turning the ropes.

"This is the *second* set of colors she's doing," her friend muttered. "Show-off."

"Mr. B said he'd take the ropes away if you don't stop now," Dee reported.

"Good." Mimi let her hands drop and the ropes went slack at one end, while the other turner kept going for a few seconds. Blanca's feet got caught in them.

"Why'd you stop?" she demanded, pouting. "I could've tripped! Besides, I had to get back to the alphabet so I could stop at C!"

Dee and Mimi rolled their eyes as they began coiling the ropes. Blanca was crazy about Casper, the most popular boy in the sixth grade. To be fair, he seemed crazy about her too, though they broke up on a regular basis.

Dee herself had always liked Casper. More than that: they shared an understanding that they had it easier than others, that they didn't have to work so hard to keep friends or be respected. The year before, she had briefly wondered if she should have a crush on him, or even take it further and go with him. Casper had an appealing, open face and bright blue eyes that put you at ease. But, though it would have been natural to, she did not think of him in that way. He was more like a brother; they were engaged in similar activities, looking forward rather than at each other. It made more sense for Casper to be with someone messy and energetic like Blanca.

"Oh my God, who's *that*?" Blanca cried. Though in class she said little, on the playground she was loud and unabashed.

Dee knew without looking that Blanca was referring to the new boy. "He's from Nigeria," she said casually, coiling the rope between her elbow and her hand.

"How do you know?" Mimi asked.

"Teachers said."

"A black boy at our school—I can't believe it!"

"Shhh . . ." Dee tried to stifle Blanca, embarrassed that the boy might hear.

She and Mimi and Blanca headed toward the lines of children, the ropes under her arm. They were kept in Mr. Brabant's room, and Dee was responsible for them—which she knew made Blanca jealous, as did her friendship with Mimi.

"Why do you like her so much when she's so weird?" Blanca had said once.

"Mimi's not weird," Dee had defended her friend. "She's ... sensitive. She feels things."

Blanca had shrugged and begun to sing "Crocodile Rock," making clear the conversation was over. Threesomes were a tricky navigation: one person was always feeling left out.

A teacher must have told the new boy where to go, for he was now standing at the end of the line that had formed in front of Mr. Brabant. Blanca came to a dramatic halt, rocking back on her heels. "Now what do we do?" she cried.

Dee hesitated, then stepped up to stand behind him. Blanca joined her and whispered loudly, "Can you believe it? He's in our class! I dare you to touch him."

"Shut up!" Dee hissed, hoping he hadn't heard. She studied his back. The new boy had the most beautifully shaped head, smooth and even and perfectly formed, like a clay pot turned on a potter's wheel. Dee wanted to reach out and cup it in her hand. His hair was cut short, like a forest of trees dotted in tight clumps over the curves of a mountain—very different from the thick Afros popular at the moment. Not that there were any Afros around to look at. There were no black students at Dee's school, or black residents in her suburban neighborhood, though by 1974 Washington, DC, itself had a large enough black population to be nicknamed Chocolate City. Sometimes when she went downtown with her family she saw black men and women with big Afros; and on TV when she watched *Soul Train* at

Mimi's house, dancing to Earth, Wind & Fire or the Jackson Five. She didn't ever see the show at home: her mother would never let her watch black people singing and dancing on TV. Dee had a crush on Jermaine Jackson, though it was his sly toothy smile she liked rather than his Afro. All of her friends preferred little Michael, who seemed to Dee too obvious a choice. It would be like choosing the cutest boy in school to have a crush on, which was perhaps why she never thought of Casper that way—and why Blanca did. Blanca always went for the obvious.

"Dee, you will look after our new student today." Mr. Brabant gestured at her from the head of the line. "Show him where the cafeteria is, the music room, the bathroom. Explain things when he doesn't understand what is going on in class. All right?"

Blanca gasped and nudged Dee, who turned red and nodded. Why had Mr. Brabant chosen her? Was he punishing her for something? Dee never needed punishing. Her mother made sure of that.

Around her, classmates were giggling and whispering.

"Where'd *he* come from?"

"The jungle!"

"Hoo-hoo-hoo . . . Ow, that hurt!"

"Don't be so immature."

"Poor Dee, having to look after him!"

"Why'd Mr. B choose her? Usually a boy looks after a boy."

"Maybe none of the boys would be willing to. I wouldn't."

"I wouldn't either!"

"Yeah, but Dee's Mr. B's pet—he knows she won't say no."

"Smart."

"Wait a minute—does this mean that that boy is going to sit at our desks?"

"Ha ha! Poor Duncan, stuck with the new boy! Patty too."

"I'll move!"

"Mr. B won't let you."

"I *will*."

"Dream on, buddy boy."

The new boy glanced behind him. His face was not wary and guarded as Dee would have expected, but open and welcoming. His eyes were black, glistening coins that regarded her with curiosity. He raised his eyebrows, widening his eyes further, and Dee felt a jolt course through her, similar to what she experienced once when she touched an electric fence for a dare.

She did not speak to him, but nodded. He returned the nod, then turned back so that he was facing forward again. They stood in line, quiet, embarrassed. Dee looked around to see if anyone was still watching them. Everyone was watching them. She settled her eyes on a house across the street from the school—Casper's house, in fact—hoping they would all assume she had her mind on important things out in the wider world rather than on the boy in front of her, who seemed to vibrate with electricity.

Then she noticed the black woman standing on the other side of the chain-link fence surrounding the playground, a hand entwined in the wire mesh. Though short, she was made taller by a red and yellow patterned scarf wrapped like a towering turban around her head. She had on a long dress made of the same bright fabric. Over it she wore a gray winter coat—even though it was early May and warm. She was watching them.

"My mother thinks that I do not know how to be the new boy."

Dee turned, amazed that he had spoken. In his place she wouldn't have said a word. "Have you been a new boy before?"

"Yes. Three times in six years. This will be my fourth school."

Dee had always lived in the same house, gone to the same school and had the same friends, and was accustomed to a comfortable familiarity underpinning everything she did. She couldn't imagine being a new girl and not knowing everyone else—though in a few months when she moved from elementary school to junior high, she would know only a quarter of the students in her grade. While in many ways Dee had outgrown her school and was ready to move on to a new one, the thought of being surrounded by strangers sometimes made her stomach ache.

Across from them in the line for the other sixth grade class, Mimi was watching this exchange, wide-eyed. Dee and Mimi had almost always been in the same class together, and it pained Dee that, this last year of elementary school, they had been assigned different teachers, so she couldn't be with her best friend all day but had to settle for playground time. It also meant Blanca, who was in Dee's class, could try to get closer—as she was now, literally hanging on Dee, a hand on her shoulder, staring at the new boy. Blanca was always physical, throwing her arms around people, playing with friends' hair, rubbing up against boys she liked.

Dee shook her off now to focus on the boy. "Are you from Nigeria?" she asked, eager to show off her prior knowledge of him. *You may be a different color,* she thought, *but I know you.*

The boy shook his head. "I am from Ghana."

"Oh." Dee had no idea where Ghana was except that it must be in Africa. He still seemed friendly, but the expression had frozen onto his face and was becoming less sincere. Dee was determined to demonstrate that she did know something about African culture. She nodded at the woman by the fence. "Is your mom wearing a dashiki?" She knew the word because for Christmas her hippie aunt had given her pants with a dashiki pattern on them. To please her, Dee had worn them at Christmas dinner, and had to endure frowns from her mother and teasing from her older brother about wearing a tablecloth when they already had one on the table. Afterward she had shoved the pants to the back of her closet and not touched them since.

"Dashikis are shirts that African men wear," the boy said. He could have been scornful or made fun of her, but instead he was matter-of-fact. "Or black Americans sometimes when they want to make a point."

Dee nodded, though she wondered what that point was. "I think the Jackson Five wore them on *Soul Train.*"

The boy smiled. "I was thinking of Malcolm X—he

wore a dashiki once." Now it seemed he was teasing her a little. Dee found she didn't mind if it meant the stiff, frozen look disappeared.

"My mother is wearing a dress made from kente cloth," he continued. "It is fabric from my country."

"Why is she wearing a winter coat?"

"Unless we are in Ghana, she feels the cold even when it is warm outside."

"Are *you* cold too?"

"No, I am not cold." The boy answered in full, formal sentences, the way Dee and her classmates did during French lessons once a week. His accent wasn't American, though it contained some American phrases. There was a hint of English in it. Dee's mother liked to watch *Upstairs, Downstairs* on TV; he sounded a bit like that, though not as clipped and expensive, and with more of a singsong cadence that must come from Africa. His full sentences and lack of contractions, the lilt in his speech, the rich exaggeration of his vowels, all made Dee want to smile, but she didn't want to be impolite.

"Is she going to pick you up after school too?" she asked. Her own mother never came to school except for parent–teacher meetings. She didn't like to leave the house.

The boy smiled again. "I have made her promise not to come. I know the way home."

Dee smiled back. "Probably better. Only the kids on the younger playground have their parents bring them to school and pick them up."

The second bell rang. The fourth grade teachers turned and led their lines of children through the entrance from the playground into school. Then fifth graders would go, and finally the sixth grade classes.

"Would you like me to carry the ropes for you?" the boy asked.

"Oh! No, thanks—they're not heavy." They were kind of heavy. No boy had ever offered to carry them for her.

"Please." The boy held out his arms and she handed them to him.

"What's your name?" she asked as their line began to move.

"Osei."

"O . . ." The name was so foreign that Dee could not find a hook in it to hang on to. It was like trying to climb a smooth boulder.

He smiled at her confusion, clearly used to it. "It is easier to call me O," he said, bringing his name into the familiar arena of letters. "I don't mind. Even my sister calls me O sometimes."

"No, I can say it. O-say-ee. Is it in your language?"

"Yes. It means 'noble.' What is your name, please?"

"Dee. Short for Daniela, but everybody calls me Dee."

"Dee? Like the letter D?"

She nodded. They looked at each other, and this simple link of letters standing in for their names made them burst out laughing. O had beautiful straight teeth, a flash of light in his dark face that sparked something inside her.

✳

Ian spotted the boy immediately, even while busy spinning the merry-go-round too fast and making the fourth graders scream. Ian would always notice anyone new who stepped into his territory. For the playground was his. It had been all year, since he had started sixth grade and there were no older boys to rule it. He'd had months to relish this domination. Any new boy posed a challenge. And *this* new boy, well . . .

Ian was not the tallest boy in the year, nor the fastest. He did not kick balls the farthest, or jump the highest when shooting baskets, or do the most chin-ups on the monkey bars. He did not speak much in class, never had gold stars pasted to his artwork, did not win certificates at the end of the year for best mathematician or best handwriting or best citizenship. Definitely not best citizenship. He was not the most popular with the girls—Casper claimed that honor.

Ian was the shrewdest. The most calculating. The quickest to respond to a new situation and turn it to his advantage. When a fight was brewing, Ian would take bets on the outcome and make sure the participants didn't chicken out. He was good at predicting who would win. Sometimes he'd bet on how long the fight would last and which teacher would break it up. He often took the stakes in candy, which he sold afterward—he did not have a sweet tooth. Sometimes he demanded others' lunch money, but other times he protected younger students from having theirs stolen, and took a cut himself. He liked to mix things up, keep kids guessing. Recently he had convinced his parents to let him open a bank account. They did not ask him how he had amassed so much money. His brothers had been the same at his age.

When his class went running around the block during PE, Ian offered to go back and collect the slower children; it gave him a chance to study what was going on out in the world during the day—who was delivering mail, who was washing their car, who was leaving their door open while they pruned their roses. Ian was always looking for the angle that would benefit him.

He did not always get it right.

A few days before, for instance, a storm had arrived out of nowhere. Ian had raised his hand while Miss Lode was trying to explain what an isosceles triangle was. She had chalk dust all over her orange pantsuit and wore a perplexed expression, as if geometry were just out of her reach too. She'd stopped, taken aback, for Ian rarely raised his hand. "Yes, Ian?"

"Miss Lode, it's starting to rain and the flag is still up. May I go take it down?"

Miss Lode glanced out the window at the amassed dark clouds and the American flag that flew all day in front of the school. "The girls in Mr. Brabant's class are responsible for it. You know that."

"They're never fast enough, though. And Mr. Brabant isn't here today to remind them. If I run now, it won't get wet."

Miss Lode hesitated, then nodded at the door. "All right, then—be quick. And take someone with you to fold it."

There were lots of rules about the American flag: it should never be flown at night or in the rain, it should never touch the ground, it should be treated with reverence. Ian had watched enviously from the window as

Dee and Blanca went to the flagpole at the beginning and end of each day, ostentatious in their privilege. Usually they worked carefully, but he had also seen them fold the flag sloppily and let a corner touch the ground. He had heard them sing songs—sometimes patriotic, but often songs from the radio. They liked to take their time, talk, dawdle, laugh.

He chose Mimi to come with him, to everyone's surprise—Miss Lode, Rod and most of the other boys, and all of the girls, who giggled behind their hands. Mimi herself looked not only amazed, but thrilled, and fearful. Until fifth grade, boys and girls had sometimes played together and declared themselves friends. But for the last two years of school, they'd separated and stayed with their own gender—unless they spent furtive moments together out of sight of the teachers, behind the gym or in the corner among the trees that provided the little shade on a sunny day. Last week Ian had draped his arm around Mimi, back behind the gym, letting his hand dangle down over her high budding breasts, but he'd been interrupted from doing more by Rod offering to drop his jeans and underwear and show what he had to the girls. Mimi had squealed along with the others and moved out from under Ian's arm—reluctantly, he sensed.

As she followed him outside to the flagpole, it was spitting with rain, though the worst of it was still up in the clouds. Ian was careful not to pay her too much attention, instead focusing on unwinding the rope from the bracket screwed onto the pole at waist height. Then he lowered the flag. "Catch the end," he commanded.

Mimi obeyed, grabbing the two corners as they came down. Ian unclipped the other two corners from the rope, then they held the flag taut between them like a sheet. Ian looked at her for a second longer than he needed to, and she stood very still, her eyes wide. They were a crystal blue swimming with dark flecks, which made them sparkle in a way that disconcerted him. She had the classic freckled skin of a redhead—Irish, probably—and a wide mouth with lips that didn't cover the braces glinting across her teeth. Her features were too irregular—her eyes too far apart, her mouth too big, her forehead broad—for her to be thought of as pretty. Nonetheless, there was something compelling about Mimi. This was their seventh year together at the same school. Ian had knocked her over once in third grade, because he could, but he had not paid much attention to her until recently. He had chosen Mimi for his focus because she was like him—a step apart from everyone else on the playground. Despite having an older and younger sister who both appeared normal, and popular Dee as her best friend, Mimi often seemed to be alone in her head, even when she was turning jump ropes or playing hopscotch. She had the reputation of being a bit out of it, of fainting at the wrong times, of saying little but watching everything. Maybe that was what appealed: he didn't want her to talk much.

He jiggled his right hand to indicate they should fold the long edge a third over; then they folded the other side on top so that the flag was a third of its width. Ian looked at Mimi too long again and she blushed. "You fold," he said. "You know how?"

Mimi nodded, and folded her end on a diagonal so that it made a triangle, then folded it again and again, getting closer with each fold. Ian held the end close to his chest so that she had to come right up to him. When she was about a foot away, ready to make the last fold, Ian tugged the flag so that she fell into him, the triangle squashed between them as he lunged for her mouth. Their teeth clattered together, and Mimi flinched, but she couldn't step back or the flag would fall to the ground.

Her braces hurt his mouth, but Ian recovered and, placing his lips firmly on hers, began to suck. After a moment Mimi responded, sucking back so that they created a vacuum and a lot of spit, though she kept her mouth too tight for him to insert his tongue. *She's done this before*, Ian realized—a thought he did not like much. He pulled away, though he had been enjoying himself and had begun to feel something, which he suspected she'd noticed. Taking the flag from her, he made the last fold and tucked the leftover cloth into two folds so that it held tight together, like the paper triangles kids made to flick across the table surface for table football. "You shouldn't be doing that with others," he said.

Mimi looked a little dazed, even frightened. "I haven't."

"You're not a very good liar. You've kissed other boys—Philip, Charlie, Duncan, even Casper." Ian was making intelligent guesses, and at least one struck home, though he didn't know which. Mimi hung her head; it was starting to rain harder, spotting her face so that it looked as if she were crying.

"If you're gonna go with me, you better not even look at those boys. Will you go with me?"

Mimi nodded.

"Then open your mouth when we kiss so I can stick my tongue in."

"The girls will be coming from Mr. Brabant's class—they'll see us."

"Nah. I've watched—they take forever to get out here. The flag always gets wet and Dee has to take it home to put it in the dryer. Come on."

He put his mouth back on hers. When she opened up, Ian thrust his tongue deep into her, backing her up against the flagpole so he could probe her teeth, her cheeks, her tongue, pumping in and out. He pushed his hips into hers to make sure that this time she definitely felt him.

When they pulled apart, they were both breathless. Kissing her made him feel light-headed and, for once, free. The rope was dangling in the rain. Ian took hold of it, glanced around, then handed the flag triangle to Mimi. "Stand back. I'm gonna show you something." Wrapping the end of the rope around his hand, he began to run, leaning out from the flagpole so that the rope was taut. Then he leaped, and swooped off the ground and out around the pole, then back in. He ran onto the ground again and then out and up—going around and around the pole. The rain fell away, Mimi, the school; all he felt was the sensation of flying.

When he lost momentum and came back down, Mimi was watching him, the flag hugged against her chest. Ian felt so good he decided to be generous. "Do you want to? Go on, it's fun." He took the flag back and handed her the rope. "Run fast, then jump."

She hesitated. "Mrs. Duke might see me. Or the teachers. We'll get caught."

Ian snorted. "No one's watching. They're too busy learning about triangles. Don't you want to?"

Mimi seemed to reach a decision, and suddenly ran and flung herself into the air, leaning away from the pole to swing around it, laughing as her feet left the ground. Ian had never seen her happier. He smiled, a quick, rare thing. When she stopped he kissed her again, this time more gently. They pulled apart just as Dee and Blanca appeared in the school entrance, to take down the flag. Dee gave them a funny look, clearly surprised to see them together, though Ian wasn't sure she had seen the kiss. It didn't matter. "You girls are way too slow," he declared, sauntering past them with the folded flag tucked under his arm. Mimi followed, her face bright red.

Unfortunately Ian had been too slow as well, for the flag was wet, which he had gone out to make sure didn't happen. Miss Lode squeezed the cloth triangle he left on her desk and frowned.

"Is that an isosceles triangle, Miss Lode?" he asked, hoping to divert her.

"Oh!" His teacher squinted at the flag. "I don't know. But that's—Jennifer, take it to Mr. Brabant's class."

"I can look after it," Ian interjected. "I can put it back up when the rain stops, and take it down at the end of the day."

"I would rather the responsibility remain with

Mr. Brabant's class. Now, go and sit down, Ian. That's enough disruption for today."

Ian kicked himself for taking the time to swing on the rope. That sensation had cost him his opportunity to gain another privilege—though he suspected that Miss Lode would always have deferred to Mr. Brabant.

The first bell rang on the playground and Ian grabbed at the bars of the merry-go-round to slow it. One of the boys riding was looking sick. Ian smirked and tugged a bar to speed it up again. "Ten cents to stop it," he called to the boy, who nodded miserably. Ian dug his feet in so that the merry-go-round came to a sudden halt. The other boys ran off toward the class lines forming at the door, relieved not to be the focus of Ian's attention this time. The unfortunate boy left behind stood still, shoulders rounded, head down.

"You pay me now," Ian said.

The boy shrugged, eyes fastened to the ground. "Don't have any money."

"You should've thought of that when you were on the merry-go-round." Ian stepped close to him. "Get back on. I'll spin you till you're sick."

"I—I'll pay you tomorrow. Promise."

"Tomorrow's no good. Now is better. What else do you have? You got any candy?"

The boy shook his head.

"Baseball cards?"

Another shake.

"Well, what do you have?"

Another shrug.

Ian riffled through the knowledge he had absorbed by watching and noting all that went on around him. "Give me the Hot Wheels you've got—the red Camaro."

He struck home, for the boy began to search his pockets. "I've got a nickel. I can give you that now, and the rest tomorrow—or after lunch. I can go home at lunchtime and get five more cents."

But Ian was already reaching for the canvas book bag the boy had flung next to the fence a few innocent minutes before, back when riding a merry-go-round seemed like something fun to do before school. Ian extracted a low red sports car with fat wheels that fit perfectly in the palm of his hand. It was still gleaming: clearly a recent acquisition. As he pocketed the car, he heard the boy mutter, "Chump."

Ian took the car back out of his pocket and let it drop, then stamped on it. The wheels snapped off, the doors popped open, the roof caved partway in, and red paint flaked off the hood. "Oops," Ian said, and left it there. A moment later he chided himself for letting his anger get the better of him and wasting a good Hot Wheels, when he had been called far worse things before than "chump." But it *was* satisfying to see the expression on the boy's face, looking even sicker than he had on the merry-go-round.

During this whole exchange Ian had kept an eye on the new arrival hovering at the edge of the playground. Now he changed direction and headed over to the new boy. To the black boy. For he was very black. Ian had picked up the information during one of his fact-finding missions that a new boy was joining the sixth grade, but he'd missed the crucial bit about his skin color. He winced inwardly as he got close and took in the dark skin, the black eyes, the sweat glistening in the hair cut close to his skull. *Take charge*, he thought. *Keep your friends close, your enemies closer.* His father liked to quote that. "You have to line up when the bell rings," he said. "Over there. You're in Mr. Brabant's class."

The boy nodded. "Thank you." Just those two words and the way he said it—straightforward, confident even, with his foreign intonation—and his subsequent walk over to the line as if he already knew the playground, and owned it, struck a match of fury in Ian's gut.

"Damn." Rod had sidled up like an uncertain dog. Small and wiry, he had dark shaggy hair to his shoulders and cheeks that reddened easily when he was upset. They were red now. "What the hell has happened to this shithole?" Ian's sidekick swore a lot around him, clearly thinking it made him sound tough. Ian himself never swore. His father had taken his belt to him early on to make clear that swearing was his domain, not his son's.

Ian had tolerated Rod for a long time but would not classify him as a friend—though he had heard Rod refer to him as his best friend, which was something only a girl would say. To Ian, Rod was merely a prop who helped him retain his playground standing, who looked out for teachers when Ian was taking bets or extracting lunch money or tormenting kids for fun. It was the plight of a sidekick to be despised by his master almost as much as by others. Rod was weak, and whiny, and desperate. He was whining now. "Look at that—she's talking to him. I'm never gonna get to go with her!"

Mimi's friend Dee had joined the line behind the black boy and was now talking to him. Ian watched them, almost impressed by Dee's boldness. When she handed the jump ropes to the boy and they began to laugh, however, Ian frowned. "Don't like that," he muttered. He would have to do something about it.

❋

Mimi was rhythmically turning the Double-Dutch ropes so that they smacked evenly on the ground. She could feel the playground around her pulsing with activity. Nearby, two girls were arguing over a hopscotch square drawn crookedly. Three boys raced the length of the playground, one of them surging past the others at the end. A girl sat on a low wall, reading a book. A line of boys, backs to the school and out of sight of the teachers, were seeing who could pee the farthest through the chain-link fence onto the sidewalk. Three girls laughed together over an Archie comic book. A boy kicked sand from the sandpit under the trees.

Two areas of activity on the playground snagged at her, two so different they balanced each other out. There was Ian on the merry-go-round, tormenting the fourth graders. Mimi already knew how this would end. She herself was on a kind of merry-go-round with him, but she did not know how that would end. While swinging around the flagpole three days before, she had been exhilarated and terrified at the same time, like going very high in a swing and then leaning backward and keeping your eyes open so that you can see as well as feel the sickening plunge as you fall backward. Since then she had felt bound to Ian, and was not sure whether or not she wanted to free herself from him.

The opposite of the rapid spin of the merry-go-round, with its riders always on the verge of being flung off, was the new boy. The new *black* boy—there was no ignoring the color of his skin—was standing absolutely still, and bringing attention to himself with his stillness. If she were a new girl Mimi would be walking all around the playground, making herself less of a target by moving among the others, trying not to linger and be noticed. Though Mimi had never been a new girl, she had never entirely belonged either. Best friend of Dee, and now girlfriend of Ian: you would think these concrete relationships would tether her, but they did not. She felt as if she were floating through the playground world.

The spinning and the stillness. The motion and the motionless. The white and the black. If ever the playground had been imbalanced, with its new addition it now had a disorienting equilibrium. Mimi shook her head to clear it.

That movement caused her arm to shake, and one of the jump ropes wobbled and caught the jumper—a fifth grader, who began to complain until Mimi stopped her with a look. She knew it was her fault the girl had been tripped up, but she did not show it, could not apologize or explain, or her reputation as the steadiest turner would suffer. The steady turner, and the girl who sensed things. She must hold on to these different gifts, for they were all she had. They, and now Ian, who was not exactly a gift.

The fifth grader skulked off, and Mimi regretted it, for Blanca took her place. Blanca, the cutest girl in the sixth grade, who lessened her looks by wearing clothes just this side of vulgar: a tight pink top that showed off every strap and outline of her training bra, a short denim skirt, beige platform sandals, red barrettes in her black hair with glittering pink jewels pasted on, half a dozen gold bangles that clinked on her arm as she jumped. And jumped, and jumped. Blanca was as steady a jumper as Mimi was a turner. They bored each other in their parts.

Mimi let her jump, kept the rhythm, and with that background thumping, watched the playground gradually turn its attention to the stranger. No one stopped what they were doing, exactly, or not for more than a startled moment, a pause during tag, a hesitation between catching a ball at jacks and throwing it up again, a silence in the midst of chatter. Then they went back to tag, to jacks, to talking, but with one eye or ear now focused on this boy. Mimi sensed the playground and its players as strings randomly crisscrossing all over it, now starting to align so that the strings led to one point. *How does he stand such attention?* she thought.

Rippling over all of those strings came Dee, with her blond hair pulled into tight pigtails braided by her mother, who believed girls should be buckled in for as long as possible. Dee was coming over to tell Mimi to stop, then would take away the ropes and go stand in line next to the new boy. She was going to focus entirely on him. Mimi already knew this was going to happen. She often knew.

She was right: Dee paid Mimi and Blanca only cursory attention before going to stand next to the new boy. Mimi went to her own line, where she couldn't help watching Dee and the boy. Everyone was watching them. The relentless curiosity made the two seem surrounded by a shimmering aura like the one Mimi sometimes saw behind her eyes when a headache was coming on. In fact, even now her head had that buzzing, attentive feeling that preceded one, like the tension in the air when a thunderstorm is brewing.

Then Dee gave the boy the precious class jump ropes, and they began to laugh, throwing their heads back as if there were no audience but the two of them, performing for each other. It was so unexpected—what student would laugh five minutes into his first day at a new school?—that Mimi found herself laughing too, in surprise, in sympathy, in imitation. She was not the only one—others were also infected, smiling and laughing because they could not help it.

Not Ian. Her boyfriend—for that was what everyone called them now, boyfriend and girlfriend—was standing off to one side, staring at Dee and the boy, a snarl pressed into his face that punctured Mimi's joy.

I can't go with him anymore, she thought. *I can't go with a boy who responds like that to laughter.* For a moment Mimi thought of the feeling of flying around the flagpole, and of Ian pushing into her with his tongue and hips, which she thought she would not like but did, surprised to find her body responding like a light being switched on. But she could not have someone like Ian turning on that light.

She pondered when to tell him she was breaking up with him. Maybe at the end of the day when she could run home afterward, and pretend to have one of her really bad headaches the next day so she wouldn't have to go to school. Tomorrow was Friday, after that the weekend, and she hoped Ian's anger might have burned itself out after three days. Then there would be only a month of school to get through before a summer away from him, and then a new school to lose herself in.

Now that she had a plan she felt better—apart from the stab of jealousy as she watched Dee and the new boy walk through the school entrance, their strides already matched the way friends and couples walk together at the same pace.

Yes, she felt better. And yet there lurked a flicker behind Mimi's eyes, and the slow grip of a vice at her temples. That would not go away until her head was taken over and she submitted to the pain, like a test she had to pass before she could be light and free again.

✳

Osei surveyed the playground with a practiced eye. He had looked over new playgrounds three times before, and knew how to read them. Every playground had the same elements: swings, slide, merry-go-round, monkey bars, jungle gym. Lines and bases painted on the asphalt for softball and kickball. A basketball hoop at one end. Space for hopscotch and jump rope. This one had two unusual features: a pirate ship with poles and rigging that could be climbed; and a sandpit edged by a clump of trees.

Then there were the kids you always saw doing the same things: the boys, running chaotically, burning up the energy that otherwise made them restless in class; or playing with a ball, always something with a ball. The girls, playing hopscotch or jacks or jump rope. The loners, reading or sitting on top of the monkey bars or tucked away in a corner or standing close to the teachers where it was safe. The bullies, patrolling and dominating. And himself, the new boy, standing still in the midst of these well-worn grooves, playing his part too.

Looking over the kids, he was also hoping to spy something else: an ally. Specifically, one of his own. Another black face or, if that wasn't available, a brown face, or a yellow face. Puerto Rican. Chinese. Middle Eastern. Anything different from the parade of pink-and-cream suburban Americans. But there was none. There rarely was. And when there was, they weren't always any help. In his London school there had been one other black student—a girl with Jamaican parents, who never once met his eyes, who stayed as far from him as she could, as if they were two magnets pushing away from each other. She had found her own precarious perch and did not want to get pulled into his struggle to find a safe place. In his New York school there had been twin Chinese brothers who when goaded would use kung fu moves in fights, which hurt their opponents but delighted the onlookers. They also kept their distance from Osei.

He had learned over time to hide what he was thinking as the new boy. His father might be the diplomat in the family, but Osei too was a diplomat of sorts, displaying his skills at each new school. Whenever his father came home from his new job and at dinner told his wife and children about all the new people he worked with and how he didn't know where to park his car or where the bathroom was, Osei could have said, "That is my day too." When his father said he forgot the name of his new secretary each time and so called them all "Miss," O could have said he'd learned that in Victorian England people called all of their female servants "Abigail" no matter what their names were, so that they didn't have to remember new ones. That he too had to rummage through all the names of adults he had stored in his head and pick out the right one for the teacher standing at the front of the class, since the formality of calling them "Sir" or "Miss" would make them raise their eyebrows and the other students laugh, and set him apart even more. That he too had a new job, which was to be the new boy and try to fit in—or not. But he didn't say any of these things. He had been taught to respect his elders—which meant not questioning or defying them. If his father wanted to know any specifics about his son's day, he would ask. And since he never did, O kept quiet.

Today he was facing yet another playground full of white kids staring at him, another bunch of boys sizing him up, another bell ringing the same pitch heard all over the world, another teacher at the head of the line eyeing him uneasily. He had been through all of this before, and it was all familiar. Except for her.

Osei felt her presence behind him like a fire at his back. He turned, and she started, casting her eyes down. She had been looking at his head. O had caught others looking at it before. It seemed his best quality was the shape of his skull, round and symmetrical, with no points or bulges. His mother liked to remind him that she gave birth to him by cesarean and so his soft skull was not squashed coming out. "Stop!" he always cried, not wanting to picture it.

When Dee—how perfect that she should be called a letter too—raised her eyes, the fire leaped and spread through him. Her eyes were brown: the clear liquid brown of maple syrup. Not the blue he'd seen on so many playgrounds, the blue of the English, the Scottish, the Irish ancestors. The blue of Germany and Scandinavia. The blue of Northern Europeans who came over to North America to settle, and conquered the brown eyes of the Indians and brought the black eyes from Africa to do their work. O looked at her with his black eyes and she answered him with brown—the brown of the Mediterranean, perhaps, of Spain or Italy or Greece.

She was beautiful—not a word anyone usually used to describe an eleven-year-old girl. "Cute" was more common, or "pretty." "Beautiful" dug deeper than a girl that age could normally stand up to. But Dee *was* beautiful. She had a cat-like face shaped by her bones—her cheeks, her temple, her jaw—angular as origami where most girls were pillow-soft. Her blond hair was French-braided into two plaits that ran down her back like ropes. O caught a whiff of her shampoo, floral with a sharp sprig of rosemary. It was Herbal Essence, a shampoo his sister, Sisi, loved but couldn't use because it didn't contain enough oil for African hair. She complained about that, and about the label with its drawing of a white woman with long blond hair, surrounded by pink flowers and green leaves. But she bought a bottle anyway, just to smell it.

The beauty of this girl standing behind him was not just physical, though. It seemed to O that she was lit from within by something most kids either did not have or hid deep inside: soul. He thought no one could ever hate her, and that was rare in this world. She was there to make things better. And she was already making things better for him: talking to him, laughing with him, responsible for him. It didn't matter that other students were staring and making fun of them. O kept his eyes on Dee and ignored the rest.

As they headed toward his new classroom, Osei knew he could ask her for help with the one small thing that was bothering him—small and concrete as opposed to the large and unfixable issue of his being the only black student at an all-white school. "Please, do you have a pencil case?" he asked.

Dee looked puzzled. "Yes, in my desk. Why? Don't you?"

"I do, but . . ." He tucked the jump ropes under one arm and unbuckled his book bag, a blessedly unremarkable dark green satchel that had seen him through three schools without drawing attention to itself. The same could not be said of the pencil case he showed Dee, pulling out just part of it so that others wouldn't see. It was a pink plastic rectangle, studded with red knobbly strawberries that protruded from the smooth surface like giant braille. O had not been able to find his own pencil case—buried in one of the boxes that had not yet been unpacked after the latest move—and his mother insisted he take the strawberry case, which had belonged to Sisi until she became too grown up for it. When O asked his mother why she thought a boy would use a pink strawberry case, she blinked and said, "Osei, a student needs a case for his pencils. I am not sending my son to school without his pencils."

He could not argue with his mother, and could not stop her from packing the case in his school bag herself, along with a handkerchief that he would never use, a sandwich he didn't know if he would need, and a can of Coke he suspected the school wouldn't allow him to drink. There was nothing useful in the bag, and yet he slung it over his shoulder and took it to school. He couldn't hide the pencil case somewhere as he'd hoped, however, for his mother accompanied him almost to the gate, even after he pleaded with her to let him go on alone. At least she didn't come onto the playground with him, though she remained by the fence, watching until he had gone inside. No one else's parents did that—not in the sixth grade.

Dee's eyes widened when she saw the strawberry case. She did not pull it out and hold it up and embarrass him in front of everyone else. Instead she reached over and touched one of the strawberries, running her finger over its pimpled surface and around its outline, just as Sisi used to do, absently fingering a strawberry while she did her homework at the kitchen table. That was before she began taking homework to her room, keeping her radio on and the door closed. Now Osei was not sure where she did her homework—or if she did it.

"It belongs to my sister," he explained, "but she no longer uses it. She is in high school. Tenth grade. They do not use pencil cases. I could not find mine and so I had to bring hers."

He fell silent, thinking about his sister. Sisi had always had his back when they were younger, defending him when they were at the same school, listening to his complaints about how his classmates treated him, reassuring him that it would get easier as he got older. They had tacitly agreed not to tell their parents, backing each other up on the lies they told to cover for stolen school bags, shirts splattered with ink, bloody lips, and, once, a hank of hair chopped from the end of one of Sisi's cornrows. (Osei had to take the blame for that, and be spanked by his father. He didn't complain.)

Once Sisi went on to junior high, though, and they were in different schools, she began to pull away from her brother and her parents. Instead of hanging out with Osei after school, she shut herself up in her room and stayed on the phone for hours, having inane conversations with friends she had just spent the whole day with. O knew they were inane because he sometimes listened in on the extension phone until he grew bored with talk about TV shows and kids in her school and crushes they had on boys and clothes they wanted to buy. At dinner Sisi talked back to her parents as much as she dared, or stuck to sullen silence—possibly a safer option around their father.

Sisi treated Osei with the condescending distance a teenage girl is so expert at. It hurt. Osei stopped telling her things that happened at school, keeping to himself his ripped shirts in Rome and knees scuffed from being tripped up in New York. Nor did he share the good things: the goals saved, the girl who talked to him, the surprised praise from a teacher for a book report on *Mrs. Frisby and the Rats of NIMH*. He figured she was no longer interested. She was not reading *The Egypt Game* or *The Wind in the Willows* or *A Wrinkle in Time*, but teenage books like *Go Ask Alice*, or books about black people: *The Invisible Man* by Ralph Ellison, *Things Fall Apart* by Chinua Achebe, *I Know Why the Caged Bird Sings* by Maya Angelou.

Their mother was sanguine about Sisi's transformation. "Osei, your sister is growing up," she soothed her son. "She does not want to have her little brother around her now. But you know that she still loves you. It will be easier for her to show it when she is older. You must be patient with her and she will come back."

Their second year in New York, when she turned fifteen, Sisi mutated into someone even more distant, to the point where he had to remind himself she was his sister. First she began dropping white friends she had in school, which left her with no friends at all since her school was all white. Then she began hanging out with black kids she'd met somewhere, and adopted an American accent sprinkled with slang. "Solid," she began to say. "Your mama," she said to insult someone. The day she referred to white people as "honkies"—though not in front of their parents—Osei knew their paths had truly diverged.

This angry black girl performance only lasted a month or two before segueing into something more sophisticated, and equally baffling to Osei. Dropping the American slang, she stepped up the singsong Ghanaian accent she and Osei had had as small children. She began wearing bright tunics made of kente cloth—to her mother's delight. Mrs. Kokote wasn't so pleased, however, when Sisi grew her hair out into an Afro so long it bowed under its own weight. When she chided her daughter, Sisi laughed and put an arm around her mother. "But *Maame*, you should be pleased that I am letting my hair go natural, the way God intended African hair to be."

She began to go out more after school and on weekends. Osei eavesdropped outside her door and learned she was lying to her parents about where she was and whom she was with. One day he secretly followed her to Central Park, where she sat with a group of other young black teenagers he didn't recognize. They were dressed similarly to Sisi, in dashikis or other tops made of kente cloth, and had big Afros. From a distance he could not hear what they were saying, but could guess from the phone calls he had listened in on: they were American but would have neo-African names they'd taken on like Wakuna, Malaika, or Ashanti, and they would sprinkle their conversation with references to Malcolm X, Marcus Garvey, the Black Panthers, slogans like Black Power and Black Is Beautiful, and terms he didn't understand like "white supremacy," "pan-Africanism," and "internalized racism." Osei watched Sisi raise her fist in the black power salute whenever anyone arrived or left—a gesture he recognized from the poster she had put up in her room of the athletes Tommie Smith and John Carlos raising their fists at the 1968 Olympics in Mexico. It made him uneasy. She was fifteen years old; wasn't that too young to become a radical? He missed their earlier ease with each other, when they used to play gin rummy or try to learn dances from *Soul Train*. He even missed her sullen teenage silence. He didn't want to hear her talking about the oppressor and the oppressed.

O snuck away from Central Park that day without revealing himself. He did not say anything to Sisi later. Nor did he tell his parents what their daughter was doing. The Kokotes seemed blissfully unaware of Sisi's new activities.

On the other hand, just before they left for Washington, his mother made him get a haircut, so that he lost his own big Afro. He'd been proud of it, carrying a pick in his back pocket everywhere he went, to comb his bush and keep it even and tidy. Osei did not normally fight with his parents, but he argued hard against getting a haircut. "Why?" he kept asking.

"There is too much emphasis on hair in this household," his mother insisted obliquely. "It is better for a fresh start."

When O continued to complain, his father cut in. "Son, you will do what your mother asks, and you will not question her judgment. She knows what she is talking about."

That was the end of the argument and the Afro. "Sorry, little brother," Sisi said when she saw him postcut. She chuckled. "You look like a sheep when it has been shorn!"

He noticed her own Afro was still intact.

Now as Osei entered the classroom alongside Dee, his new teacher had another student move so that they could sit together at a cluster of desks, which were grouped in fours, facing each other so they made rectangles. This was clearly an unusual decision, as O could hear murmurs ripple through the classroom until the teacher cleared his throat and all went quiet.

"Do you have pencils and pens and a ruler and eraser?" he demanded of his new student.

Osei froze, not wanting to pull out the strawberry case, for he could predict the teasing that would follow, but he was not sure what else to do. Dee knew, though. Reaching into her desk, she drew her own case onto her lap, then slid it over into his without anyone seeing.

"Yes . . ."

"Mr. Brabant," Dee whispered.

"Mr. Brabant." O held up the case. It was white, which was not a color he would have chosen, but at least it wasn't pink. It had Snoopy on it, the dog from the Charlie Brown comic strip, sitting on his red doghouse, hunched over a typewriter. Snoopy was all right; O preferred him to miserable Charlie Brown or bossy Lucy. Reasonable Linus would have been acceptable too, or Schroeder playing his piano. Snoopy, though, had one advantage over all of them: he did not have white skin, but black and white fur.

Across the room one of the girls—a pretty one made ugly by trying too hard with her clothes—openly gasped, clearly recognizing Dee's case.

Mr. Brabant, however, was not the sort of teacher who would get to know every student's pencil case. He merely nodded and began to call the roll. Dee's last name was Benedetti. O had been right—Italian. Many of the others were the common American last names like Cooper, Brown, Smith, Taylor. But there were plenty of immigrant names as well: Fernandez, Korewski, Hansen, O'Connor. Despite the eclecticism of those names, his own name, Osei Kokote, which Mr. Brabant wrote in at the end of the roster, still stuck out.

When the teacher's back was turned, O handed back the Snoopy case. Then he took everything out of the strawberry case. "You have it," he whispered, and set it in her lap.

"Ohhh," Dee breathed. "Are you sure?"

"Yes."

"Thank you!" She smiled and began transferring her pencils to the strawberry case. Then she held out the empty Snoopy to him. "Let's trade."

"You do not have to do that," O whispered.

"I want to. I love it." Dee squeezed his sister's case and continued to hold out hers. "I want you to have mine."

O took the Snoopy case. The girl sitting across from Dee—straight mousy-brown hair, with carefully trimmed bangs crossing her forehead, and wearing a plaid pinafore dress—was watching their transaction with fascination, unable to hide her disgust. O widened his eyes at her, and she dropped her own and reddened.

"That's Patty," Dee said. "And Duncan." She nodded at the stocky boy across from him, who was catching the eyes of friends in other clusters around the room and trying not to laugh. O fixed his gaze on him, and when at last they made eye contact, Duncan stopped smiling.

Osei packed his things into Dee's case, though now that they had made the swap he felt a little regretful about giving away something of his sister's. The strawberry case had accompanied them to so many places, and had been a familiar sight on whatever kitchen table Sisi had done her homework on. During summer vacations she had even taken it to Ghana, where it was coveted by the cook's daughters she played with. Really it should go to them, though perhaps they were too old to care about such a thing now. Still, it felt like losing a little piece of family history.

Now Dee was running her fingers around each strawberry, just the way Sisi had. O liked to see her doing that. And when she smiled at him with her welcoming face, the fire he had felt when he first saw her flared up again.

PART II

MORNING RECESS

O and Dee, sittin' in a tree
K-I-S-S-I-N-G
First comes love, then comes marriage
Then comes Dee with a baby carriage!

Blanca made a beeline for Mimi as she came onto the playground at recess. Mimi's head was still reeling from the Xs and Ys Miss Lode had introduced them to that morning. "Technically you don't start algebra until eighth grade," she'd announced. "But seventh-grade math will include some elements of algebra, and I don't want my students from this school looking blank when your future teachers begin to teach it. Besides, Mr. Brabant has already begun having his students work on equations. You don't want to be left behind."

Miss Lode was sensitive to the perception that the other sixth grade class, with its more experienced teacher and bright students like Patty and Casper and Dee, was more advanced than hers. Mimi could have told her, though, that for every Patty in Mr. Brabant's class, there was also a Blanca: Blanca with her tight top and her lips stained red from the Now and Later candy she'd been sneaking during class. Her breath smelled of synthetic cherry as she grabbed Mimi and cried, "Dee gave her pencil case to the new boy—I saw him with it!"

"What—Snoopy?" Like many girls, Mimi could

itemize her friends' wardrobes and possessions, especially the things she coveted: Blanca's polka-dot flamenco shoes, Dee's owl necklace, her older sister's shiny red raincoat. She knew who had the Partridge Family lunch box, the pencils with tiny troll erasers on top, the smiley-face pin. Of course she knew what Dee's pencil case looked like, just as Dee would know hers was made of old jeans and had a pocket on the outside where Mimi kept an emergency wintergreen Life Saver.

"I couldn't believe it!" Blanca rested her arm on Mimi's shoulders as if they were best friends. She always assumed an intimacy that the other girls did not feel.

Mimi moved out from under Blanca's arm. "So what's Dee going to use instead for a pencil case?"

Blanca shrugged. "No idea. And they were sitting together, and talking the whole time! I bet they held hands under the desk."

"Did you bring the ropes?"

"Dee'll bring them. Let's go wait on the ship."

The pirate ship was made of wood, with a cabin to wriggle through and a deck tilted as if it were sailing through a stiff wind. There was a tall mast and a crow's nest at the top, which you could climb up to on rigging or using a rope ladder. It had been built in honor of Mrs. Hunter, the school principal for twenty-five years, who had retired a few years before. The girls liked to lie in a row on the sloping deck, propping their feet up on the cabin and seeing who could blow the biggest bubbles with their gum. They weren't allowed to chew gum in class, so they waited till they got to the ship to cram their mouths with pieces of Big Buddy bubble gum, in pink and red and purple. Only Mimi couldn't, as gum got stuck in her braces.

Two fourth grade boys were climbing on the rigging, but took one look at Mimi and Blanca and jumped off. Mimi sighed as she settled on the deck. "We'll be the youngest in the playground next year," she said, closing her eyes and turning her face toward the sun. "There isn't even anything to play on in the junior high playground. No swings, no slide, no ship. I bet they don't jump rope either."

"True. But I'm ready." Blanca snapped her gum and drummed her long bare legs against the deck. "I'm sick of this school. I wanna meet new people."

Mimi smiled, her eyes still closed. "New boys, you mean."

"It's *Dee* who's got the new boy. I'm not sure I'd want him." Blanca made it sound as if she could've had him if she chose to.

"Why not? You don't even know what he's like."

"I know, but . . . it would be strange."

Mimi opened her eyes and looked at Blanca. "What would be strange?" She enjoyed watching Blanca squirm.

"Well, like, what would it be like touching his hair? Isn't it—greasy or something?"

Mimi shrugged. "Does it matter? Do you touch Casper's hair?" Blanca had been going with Casper on and off all year; Mimi wasn't sure if they were on or off now. It usually depended on how irritated Casper got with Blanca's attention—though when they were on they seemed to be more genuine than any of the other "couples" who had tried going together. They certainly seemed more real than she and Ian did.

"It would still be weird." Blanca blew a pink bubble and let it collapse over her generous lips.

"Maybe he'd think *you're* weird."

"*I'm* not weird! *You're* the one who's weird!"

Their bickering could have escalated, but Dee joined them then and they directed their attention to her. "Where are the ropes?" Blanca demanded.

"Oh. I forgot." Dee looked dazed, as if she had just been asleep.

Blanca began to laugh. "I can't believe you forgot! Somebody's in *loooooove*."

Mimi glanced over at the jump rope area, where the pavement was smooth. It was already full, with two single ropes and a Double Dutch squeezed in. Two of the groups were fifth graders that they could kick off if they wanted to. But Dee was settling down next to them, and neither she nor Blanca looked eager to go back inside and get the ropes. "Sorry I'm late," she said. "I was showing Osei where the boys' bathroom is."

"Osei?" Mimi repeated.

"The new boy. He said we can call him O. I've been looking after him this morning. Though he doesn't really need it—he's used to new schools. He's been to three other schools in the last six years."

"What's he like?"

"Really nice. Really. And smart. He's from Ghana, by the way. I got that wrong before. Did you hear his accent? It's so cute. I could listen to him all day."

She's got it bad, Mimi thought. "Why's he in DC?"

"His father is a diplomat and got posted to the embassy downtown."

"But why now? The school year will be over in a month. It doesn't seem worth it to go through being a new boy for so little time when he'll just have to start all over again at a new school in September."

"He said his parents thought he should meet kids here, at a smaller school, even for a few weeks, so that he'll know a few people when he starts junior high."

"That's crazy," Blanca interjected. "Who'd want to be the new boy twice?" But she was already losing interest, her eyes on Casper, who was passing the ship holding a big red rubber ball. "Casper, you want to join us?"

Casper smiled at them; his easy grin, combined with his wavy shoulder-length blond hair and sky-blue eyes, made him by far the best-looking boy on the playground. "Can't—we're playing kickball. See you later."

"I hope your team wins!"

Mimi glanced at Dee so they could roll their eyes at how stupid Blanca sounded. But Dee had her eyes fixed on the entrance. "I hope Osei didn't get lost. Otherwise he'll be too late to play kickball."

Mimi grimaced. Everything Dee did and said would now be related back to the new boy; she would mention him whenever she could, eager to say his name aloud, savoring its special meaning while all around her remained ignorant of the effect. That too was part of the deliciousness, that it was a secret. Even Mimi had briefly fallen for it, using Ian's name more than she normally would after their moment together by the flagpole.

Here came O now, passing the ship as if in slow motion, turning his head and smiling at Dee as if she were the only girl on the playground. Mimi had a strong sense of being excluded, like standing on the outside of a beautiful walled garden. It made her want to growl like a cat. *I should try to be nice about him,* she scolded herself. *Dee's my friend, even if she's going to spend all her time with him now.*

She looked over at the boys, swarming like bees around Ian and Casper in the corner of the playground. Kickball was one of the few games boys and girls played together, but there were unwritten rules about it that no one questioned. At morning recess only the boys played; in the afternoon girls could as well.

"I bet Ian will choose O for his team," she offered. But saying Ian's name now did not make her glow, as Dee clearly did saying the new boy's. Mimi and Ian had only been going together for three days, but already she knew she should get out of it. Her stomach hurt when she thought about her plan to dump him at the end of the school day. He was one of those boys who never forgot if he was slighted, who would await his opportunity for revenge, even if it took years. She wasn't sure now that she could break up with him. She might have to wait for him to get tired of her, and she had no idea how long that would take.

Only one good thing had come out of going with him. Mimi still revisited the sensation of flying around the flagpole at the end of the rope. Whatever else Ian made her feel now, at least he had given her that moment of freedom.

"Casper might choose Osei for his team instead," Dee said.

"We're not gonna sit here and watch the boys play, are we?" Blanca complained. "So boring! I'd rather watch the Double Dutch." She hopped off the ship and headed toward the jump rope area. Blanca was always good at worming her way in; eventually she would get a turn. Mimi's eyes followed her, tempted.

"Doesn't O have the most beautifully shaped head?" Dee announced. "And his eyes—when he looks at you he's really *looking* at you, you know?"

"I didn't notice." Actually Mimi had noticed. "Blanca told me you gave him Snoopy."

"Yes, we swapped. He gave me a pink case with strawberries on it. It's so sweet, you'd love it. And so generous of him."

Mimi considered pointing out that trading was not necessarily that generous since he was getting something too, but thought the better of it. She started to get to her feet. Watching Double Dutch was definitely preferable to listening to Dee talking about the new boy.

"Don't go." Dee put her hand on Mimi's arm. "I really think you'll like O. When we had geography this morning we were filling out maps of the world with capital cities, and I got to do it with him. He did it so fast, and got them all right. Do you know he's lived in Rome? And London. And Accra in Ghana, and now here. That's four capitals he's lived in! Plus New York."

"Does he speak Italian?" Mimi was interested despite herself.

"I didn't ask, but I will if you want. I'm so glad he's here. I like him more than I've ever liked a boy before."

"Dee, he's black." In her irritation Mimi was more blunt than she'd intended, but she wanted to shake up her friend—and punish her, a little, for abandoning her for a boy.

Dee snorted. "So?"

"So . . . doesn't that matter to you?"

"Why should it matter?"

"Because he's different from us. He stands out." Mimi wasn't sure why she was saying this; she wasn't even sure she believed it. She was aware too that she sounded just like Blanca a few minutes before. But she persisted; she wanted to warn her friend of what she sensed lay ahead. "People will make fun of you. Going with a monkey, they'll say. Not *me*, of course, but others."

Dee stared at her. "Are you kidding me? That's all you've got to say about him? You want to tell me he's too different to go with?"

"No, I . . . Forget I said anything. I'm your best friend, I just want to make sure you don't get hurt—not by *him*, but—"

"His name is Osei, Mimi. Why don't you call him by his name?"

"OK, *Osei*. He seems nice enough. But you're gonna get a lot of hassle if you go with him. And what would your mom say? She'd have a fit!"

Dee turned pale at the mention of her mother, then covered it with defiance. "I don't care what other people think—or my mother. And I like him *because* he's different."

The boys had split into teams now and started playing kickball. Dee had her eyes on O, out in the field toward the back. "You know," she added, "I could've said things about you going with Ian, but I didn't."

I probably deserved that, Mimi thought. "I'm sorry," she said. "I was just trying to help. Don't be mad at me."

"I'm not. I *could* be, 'cause what you said could be offensive—to Osei as well as to me. But I know you didn't mean it. Don't worry, I can take care of myself." Dee's string of adult sentiments sounded unconvincing to Mimi, and condescending. But she merely nodded, relieved her friend wasn't angry. Dee was too smitten to be.

As she turned to watch Ian roll the ball toward the first kicker, Mimi could feel the tension building in her head and her gut. Eventually it would have to be released.

❋

Osei was relieved when the bell rang for morning recess. Although a classroom was safer—he had his desk, his place where he was meant to be; and he had his tasks, what he was supposed to do; and best of all he had Dee paying attention to him—after an hour and a half the room had become oppressive and he was ready for fresh air, whatever dangers the playground held.

The classroom was like the others he had been a student in—though maybe more liberal than the English and Italian schools. There was schoolwork on all the walls: an art project where students drew self-portraits; posters about photosynthesis, pandas, Australia, Martin

Luther King Jr. There were pieces of rock on the windowsill: quartz, marble, granite, lava. There was a whole wall about the Apollo space missions, and a reading corner full of cushions and beanbags, where you could go if you'd finished your work. The walls there were covered with posters of peace signs and the Beatles' *Yellow Submarine* album cover. Dee whispered that it had been set up by a teaching assistant enthusiastic about an idea called the "open classroom," but that Mr. Brabant disapproved of the corner, calling her a hippie radical behind her back, and he only let students use it on the afternoons when the assistant was there.

Mr. Brabant's desk was at the front of the class, and he sat behind it like a soldier at attention, which made all the students sit straight and still as well. He wore a suit and tie and seemed no-nonsense. Osei preferred that in teachers; you knew where you were when they were strict. It was when they tried to be your friend that misunderstandings arose. On the other hand, Mr. Brabant's cool gaze was not welcoming, but wary, as if he were waiting for O to do something he could punish him for. Osei was familiar with that drill; he would have to watch himself.

Once Mr. Brabant had quizzed Osei about his pencil case and he had quietly traded with Dee, the teacher said, "All right, class," and everyone stood and faced the corner by the door where an American flag hung. Placing their right hands on their left chests over their hearts, they began to recite: "I pledge allegiance to the flag of the United States of America ..." Dee glanced at him, but visibly relaxed when Osei began to say the words along with the others. He managed to suppress the smile that threatened to undermine the solemnity of the oath. O had never had to perform such a patriotic act in schools outside of the US—though he did once sing "God Save the Queen" at a cricket match at Lord's in London, which he'd gone to with his father. No one ever questioned reciting the Pledge of Allegiance—except for a faction of students in his school in New York who complained that having to say "one nation, under God" violated their civil rights as atheists. Osei had kept quiet while that argument went on—he didn't need to bring more negative attention to himself. Besides, his mother would have cried if she'd heard him calling himself an atheist—once he'd found out what it meant. O himself was not sure about God; in church His existence made sense, but when he was being held down and punched just out of sight of his school, he wondered then where God was.

Later when he told his sister, Sisi, what the atheists had said, she grunted. "They want to know about civil rights, they shoulda asked you." At the time she was going through the phase where she tried to sound more black American than African, with a higher tone, looser grammar, and vowels that took their time. Osei had not yet felt ready to follow her there, though he could sound American when he wanted to. Since they had spent their first years in Ghana, as well as every summer, they could turn the accent on and off like a faucet, unlike their parents. It came in handy sometimes.

O had already decided he would emphasize the African at this Washington school. White people seemed to feel less threatened by Africans. Not always, of course. But he sensed their fear about black Americans—who found ways to take advantage of that fear. It seemed to be the only advantage they had.

After the Pledge of Allegiance, Mr. Brabant handed Dee a red, white, and blue cloth triangle, and she briefly disappeared with another girl, first whispering, "I have to go put up the American flag. I'll be right back." Osei had no idea what she meant, but the moment she was gone he felt much more exposed. Around him he could hear whispers and giggles, which he tried to ignore. Across from him, Patty was peeking out from under her bangs, and turned red when he caught her at it. Next to her, Duncan stared more openly, with a puzzled expression, as if he were trying to work up a good joke about O, and failing because he wasn't quite smart enough—and knew it.

O didn't want to admit it, but it was a relief when Dee slipped back into her seat beside him.

Though Mr. Brabant was strict, throughout the morning he allowed Dee to explain things to O in a low voice. She was clearly a favorite—a teacher's pet, they called it in America. O had never been a teacher's pet, as they never really knew what to make of him. He was conscientious enough: he did his homework, he paid attention in class, he didn't misbehave. He didn't raise his hand much either, or write any particularly interesting stories, or paint a good picture, or read books above his ability. Due to moving so much, he often had gaps in his knowledge that regularly tripped him up. He was a solid B student.

O suspected his teachers were relieved that he didn't draw attention to himself by acting up or flunking or being a star student. Clearly some of them expected bad behavior. They would have been a little nervous of a black boy giving them a hard time, but others may have wanted him to, so that they could punish him. Sometimes they were taken aback by O scoring 100 percent on a pop quiz in math, or knowing that bronze was made of tin and copper, or that Berlin had a wall dividing it in two. They shot him looks that revealed suspicions he was cheating somehow, though actually he had gained much of his knowledge from overhearing Sisi as she did her homework.

Other times, though, he got tripped up on the easiest things: not knowing who the two main generals were in the American Civil War, or who had assassinated Abraham Lincoln, or that John Hancock had an elaborate signature. His method of long division was English and looked very different from the American way—though he still got the same answer. When he made mistakes, Osei sensed the teachers nodding to themselves, secretly pleased. *This* was what they expected—a black boy messing up.

After an hour the class suddenly rose collectively to its feet, carrying Osei along with it. A middle-aged woman had appeared in the doorway. She had gray hair cut like a helmet, and was wearing a dark green skirt suit and a strand of chunky fake pearls. Authority emanated from her, and Osei knew she must be the principal, come to have a look at him.

"Mrs. Duke," Dee whispered.

"Good morning, students," she said.

"Good morning, Mrs. Duke," they repeated in an obedient singsong Osei had heard in every school.

"You may sit down. I'm here to say hello to our new student, Osei Kokote." She got his last name right but pronounced his first "Oss-I," with a thick, deliberate emphasis, as if saying such a name required effort. O was not about to correct her.

"Oss-I is from Ghana, is that right, Oss-I?" Her eyes landed just above his head.

"Yes, madam," he replied automatically.

"Mrs. Duke," Dee whispered again.

"Well, Oss-I, would you like to stand and tell us something about Ghana?" Though her voice rose at the end, this was clearly a command rather than a question.

"Yes, Mrs. Duke." Osei stood. He wasn't as worried as he might be; he'd had to do this before.

"Ghana is a country in West Africa," he began, "situated between Togo and the Ivory Coast, with a coastline on the Atlantic Ocean. It has a population of nine million people. Its capital is Accra, which is where I was born. It was a colony of Great Britain until 1957, when it declared independence—the way America did in 1776," he added, because he could see the other students looking baffled. "General Acheampong led a military coup d'état in 1972 and became leader." Osei remembered the tension that summer when they returned to Ghana—tanks and soldiers with machine guns at the airport. They did not stay in Accra but went straight to his grandfather's village, where things were as they had always been.

More bafflement. The US had never had a *coup d'état,* so how could they know? O returned to more familiar topics. "Ghana has a tropical climate: it is warm all year around, and there is a rainy season in the spring and summer. Its main products are cocoa, gold, and oil."

He stopped, looking at Mrs. Duke to gauge whether she expected him to continue. He hated reducing his vibrant, complicated country to a few bland sentences. But he knew that was what she wanted.

The class was silent. Mr. Brabant was looking out the window and frowning. But Mrs. Duke nodded, satisfied. "Very good, Oss-I. That was very articulate. I always welcome the opportunity for a new student in this school to teach something to others about the world." She turned to the class. "I hope you will welcome Oss-I so that he will feel at home for the month he is here."

If only she had stopped there.

"He may not have had the opportunities that you all enjoy at our school, so I hope you will give him every chance to take part in all we have to offer to less fortunate students."

The last three words made Osei grit his teeth. Mrs. Duke's comment reminded him of a short story by Shirley Jackson called "After You, My Dear Alphonse," where a mother reveals her prejudice to the black friend her son brings home. Earlier that year, a well-meaning teacher in New York had had Osei's class read and discuss it, thinking they were old enough to handle the topic and that it might help with "interpersonal relations," as she'd put it. Instead his classmates had been awkward around him for weeks afterward.

The principal nodded at Mr. Brabant. "Thank you, class. You may continue your lesson." After she'd gone, her perfume—floral, too sweet—lingered.

When the bell rang and Dee whispered, "Morning recess," O let out a breath he hadn't realized he'd been holding in. Still, he took his time going outside, heading first to the bathroom—led there by Dee, who seemed reluctant to leave him even when he insisted he knew his way to the playground. "Your friends will be waiting for you," he said.

She shrugged. "They can wait."

"They will talk about you."

She laughed.

"Really," he said finally. "I will be fine. Please go."

Then she blushed, but she went. The moment she was gone, O wished she were back again. It was flattering to have someone be so intent.

To his relief the bathroom was empty, but he still used a stall rather than the urinal so that if anyone came in he wouldn't have to endure the pointed glances to see how big and what color his equipment was.

Stepping onto a playground as a new boy for the second time was harder than the first, where an element of surprise usually carried him through to the safe harbor of a desk. Now, as he passed out of the building and onto the playground, Osei knew people would be waiting for him, watching to see what he did, making as clear as possible that he was not like them.

It was a very different feeling from that which he had each summer as he arrived with his family at the airport in Accra, stepping outside into an intense heat that made sweat break out on his scalp. Apart from the chaos of people and cars, the honking of ubiquitous horns, the taxi drivers hissing to get their attention, the highs and lows of the surrounding voices, the shrieks and cries of a society that did not muffle how it felt, Osei always sensed something much more profound: the ease of being among people who looked like him. His people, who did not stare at him or pass judgment on his skin color. Of course, they might soon judge him on other things—humans could not help but compare—clothes, money, what you studied in school, what your father did and how you spoke and where you went on vacation and how you wore your hair. But that first immediate sense of belonging—and of being anonymous among similar skin tones—was one that Osei welcomed every summer and missed for the rest of the year.

He stood on the playground and watched as blue eyes turned toward him, as conversations died down, as the air thinned so that everything came into too sharp a focus on him.

Not for long, though. As was often the case, sports saved him. Osei was much more confident with balls and bases and goals and teams than with times tables, pop quizzes, and timelines of American history. Sports was a language he was fluent in, because it didn't require learning new things each time he moved. Cricket and softball had their differences, but swinging a bat or catching a ball or running—these movements transferred easily.

The sixth grade boys were gathering at one end of

the playground to play kickball. Osei knew it would be best to join them; taking part was a safer option than remaining alone. He had learned to play soccer in Ghana and Rome, cricket in London, softball and basketball in New York. Kickball was like softball, or English rounders, with bases and runs and outfielders and a pitcher who rolled a red rubber ball the size of a basketball at you, and you kicked it and ran. It was hard to take a bouncy ball seriously, and the kicks made everyone look a little foolish. But it was fun to play, and you didn't have to be really good to kick the ball, or catch it. Everyone stood a chance of playing well. Even American girls played kickball, whereas O had never seen Italian or English girls playing soccer.

He was not worried about the game itself, but the choosing of teams was like the cold shower he had to run through to get to the warm swimming pool. As the new boy, he was likely to be chosen last, since he was an unknown quantity and had no alliances to count on. It was always humiliating to stand there as boys were chosen, bodies thinned from either side of him till he stood with just one or two others—the weak, the sick, the friendless. The black. Usually he fixed his eyes on something in the distance so he would not have to see the grins and—worse—the looks of pity. If the captains were merciful they didn't linger, but divided up the re-jects swiftly. Sometimes, though, a captain would take his time to study who was left, and would laugh and say something derogatory to his teammates, and O would have to stand there and clench his fists and imagine his mother saying, "No violence, Osei. Fighting is not the way." He did not always obey her.

Today he stood to one side, resigned to waiting for the endgame with the other losers. At least he had something to look at in the distance: Dee was sitting with her friends on the playground pirate ship, smiling at him.

He was smiling back when he felt a nudge. "Hey," said a heavy boy next to him. "Ian wants you."

O looked up, surprised. The two captains, Casper and Ian, had each picked a teammate and were starting the second round. Ian was the boy who had told O where to stand before school. His eyes were gray like slate, with a guardedness that made it hard to read him. Osei understood that shuttering of the eyes; he had done the same himself, for protection. He was doing it now.

"You—what's your name?" Ian asked.

Osei hesitated. *I am named after Asante kings*, he wanted to say. *My name means "noble."* But he said neither of these things, though he was proud of his name. It was because he was proud of it that he wanted to keep it safe from bullies and jokers. "Call me O," he said.

"O, have you played kickball before?"

"Yes—in New York."

There was a silence. He'd noticed that the mention of New York often inspired awe from residents of other cities, who thought it was huge and dangerous. He wasn't going to tell them that he'd gone to a sedate private school—also all white—rather than a much tougher public school. Casper, the other captain, nodded in a show of respect. Osei recognized his type. He looked a little like a blond David Cassidy from *The Partridge Family*; Sisi had kept a poster of him on her wall for a few years, before replacing it with one of Malcolm X.

"All right," Ian said then, and gestured with his head for O to join him.

"What's he up to?" the heavy boy muttered to his neighbor as Osei walked awkwardly over to Ian's team, feeling the pressure of fifteen pairs of eyes on him.

It was only when he had joined them that Ian said, "Black people are good at sports, right?"

The other boys whistled through their teeth and laughed.

Osei didn't grimace, or hit him, or walk away. Here was a straight talker. It was almost a relief to hear the prejudice out in the open. Now he could be open too. "*This* black boy is," he said.

He was going to have to kick the hell out of that ball.

They lost the toss, so Ian's team fielded first. Ian didn't assign positions, but O automatically headed to the outfield where there was less action, knowing not to show off by taking first base or shortstop. He was content to wait it out in the long grass with the weaklings.

Like softball, kickball had four bases, and you had to go around them all to score a run. You were out if the fielders threw the ball you'd kicked to the base you were running to before you got there, or if you got tagged with the ball before you got to a base, or if you kicked the ball up and a fielder caught it before it touched the ground. If a team got three outs, it was the other team's turn. Whichever team scored the most runs won.

A boy named Rod was first. He kicked the ball low

and hard so that it shot between first and second bases to the fumbling outfielder on Osei's left—a slow boy who grabbed at the ball and threw it so wildly it went to O rather than toward the infield. By the time he'd scooped it up and thrown it in, Rod had reached second base. There were groans from the team and a "Come on!" from Ian, but at least they were not directed specifically at O. There was nothing he could have done better.

It felt good to have touched the ball, though. After the first touch he always felt more confident.

The next boy kicked it short and high and Ian, who was pitching, caught it easily. One out. The boys after that did what any sensible player would do and took advantage of the weakest point of the team: they aimed deliberately at the boy on Osei's left. The first time they did so the ball was on the other side of the slow boy—too far away for Osei to help him out—and the first baseman had to run and get it. Rod got to third base on that turn, and the kicker to first. The next kick, though, was high and hard and the weak boy stood under it with his arms wide, hopeful that he would miraculously discover his athletic ability and close his arms around the ball at just the right moment. Osei could have shoved him out of the way and caught the ball himself—there was plenty of time to make this calculation. But he didn't: it felt wrong to muscle in on the weak boy, and it might not help either of them. So he ran over, stood, and watched the ball drop through the boy's arms. Then he picked it up and threw it hard to second, where the baseman managed to tag the runner out. Second out, though Rod had run home to score.

That left just one runner on first when Casper stepped up to kick. Some boys you know right away will do well, even if you've never seen them perform before. Osei and the rest of the fielders took several steps back, out of respect for Casper's ability, knowing he would kick it the hardest yet. He was honorable as well: he was not going to kick the ball toward the weak kid. O glanced over at the ship and saw that the girls were watching Casper, and felt a pang that someone else was getting all the attention, even a nice kid like Casper. Ian rolled the ball to him and Casper kicked it—high, high into the air, spinning and spinning and descending toward O. He hardly had to move—just a step forward to meet it and the ball landed hard in his arms, stinging his cheeks and thumping his chest, but he held on to it and didn't let go and Casper was out.

Shouts erupted from his team. "Way to go, O!" someone called. Then he was carrying the ball toward Ian who was nodding and people were shouting his name and in the distance the girls were cheering and for a brief moment O shed the hyperawareness of his black skin and was just another shiny new hero on the playground.

As he passed by to go out to pitch, Casper said, "Nice catch." There was no layer of jealousy or sarcasm beneath his words; he meant what he said. His straightforwardness and natural self-confidence were appealing. They also made O want to trip him up.

Osei did not assume that one good catch would make him the star of the team, nor that Ian would put him in one of the best positions in the running order of kickers: fourth or fifth, when the bases might be loaded and one good kick would bring in several runs.

And he didn't do that. "You can obviously throw and catch," Ian said as the team gathered at home plate. "But can you kick?" He gave O a long look with his murky gray eyes that were set so close together you felt off-kilter looking into them. Then he gestured to the plate, and O realized he was expected to go first.

It was not a crazy tactic. If you didn't know how well someone would perform, you could take a chance on them going first and getting out and the team would still have more opportunities to score. Of course, if the first boy went up and kicked the ball far, that was a great waste, as he wouldn't bring in any runs other than his own.

And that was what Osei was going to do. What he *had* to do. He couldn't show he could throw and catch well and then kick poorly. He couldn't even kick medium-well—enough to get to first base. He had to kick a home run.

As he walked up to the plate he heard a murmur cross the playing field, and was gratified to see the fielders all take several steps back. They were expecting great things of him. Dee and Mimi were now standing on the ship, watching. In fact, it felt as if the whole playground had come to a halt.

At the school in Rome, Osei had often been the goalkeeper when they played soccer; the other boys didn't like having physical contact with black skin, and for the most part that could be avoided if he was in goal. In that position he had at least learned how to kick high and far. Normally a goalkeeper kicks a ball from stand-still, so when Casper rolled the ball toward O unexpectedly fast, he took a split second to gauge it, then ran to meet it, and felt his toe connect, true and hard. It should go far.

It did go far. The ball soared over the heads of all the fielders, flew over the chain-link fence that bounded the playground, and bounced off the roof of a blue Oldsmobile Cutlass Supreme parked across the street. A cheer rose from the field, from the girls, from the whole playground—except for Osei's team members. They groaned.

He looked around, puzzled by their response. "Is that not a home run?"

"It doesn't count if it goes out of the playground," Ian explained.

"Yeah," Duncan added, "and we can't play anymore if it does. Teachers' rule. They hate having to go after it. Look, it's gone all the way to Maple."

The ball had rolled down the street, knocking into the wheels of parked cars, and was heading into an intersection, where drivers swerved and honked.

"I am sorry. I did not know."

"You know you bounced it off of Casper's parents' car," Ian added. "He lives right across the street."

"Oh! I will apologize."

Ian shrugged. He seemed more amused at O's humiliation than angry that the game was over.

Not for long. Dee came running over from the ship. When she reached Osei she threw her arms around him. "That was amazing!"

O froze, and the rest of the kids on the playground did too: the cheers died, the buzz was silenced. Ian stopped smiling.

"She *touched* him!" Patty whispered in a mixture of awe and horror. A chorus of voices joined her.

"Not just touched—she *hugged* him!"

"Damn!"

"I wouldn't do that—would you?"

"Do you think they're going together?"

"They must be."

"She could have any boy she wants and she chooses *him*?"

"Is Dee crazy or something?"

"I don't know—he *is* kind of cute."

"Are you kidding? He's—you know!"

"Not only that—he's *new*. She doesn't even know him."

"Yeah, he could be an axe murderer, or like that guy dressed as Santa who strangles the girl in *Tales from the Crypt*."

"You saw that? My parents wouldn't let me."

"I saw *The Exorcist* too. Snuck in with my older brother. Scared the hell out of me—especially that weird voice she talked in."

Osei could not hear what they said, but it didn't matter. They were all witnesses to a line he had never intended to cross.

❋

Dee noticed when she was hugging him that Osei stiffened, and when she pulled away from his smooth arms she became aware of the rigid atmosphere around them. Mimi had her eyes fixed on the ground; the boys—Ian and Casper and Rod and the others—stood straight as soldiers, arms at their sides. Patty was shaking her head slightly. Dee had touched O, in front of everyone, and the disapproval of the entire playground and even, it seemed, of O himself, was so strong that she had to close her eyes to it. "Let's go to the trees," she said. Sanctuary.

The cypress trees were the most surprising feature of the playground. The designer must have had a soft spot for trees, and instead of tearing out the existing stand of cypress trees when the school was being built, they were left, the playground designed around them so that they towered over one corner. Perhaps to justify keeping them, a sandpit had been built there, which was never used for play—this was the older students' playground, and digging in sand was something only younger kids did with any enthusiasm. Instead it became one of the few neutral places on the playground where boys and girls from all the grades went to hang out.

Dee led O to the trees and dropped to the sand. He hesitated, then joined her. As they sat side by side, the playground slowly began to revive. The boys got the kickball back and used it to play dodgeball—Ian and Rod throwing particularly hard and making red marks on the calves of the boys who wore shorts. Girls got on with hopscotch, and Mimi sat playing jacks with her classmate Jennifer not far from the sandpit. Blanca had begun jumping Double Dutch.

"That was such a great kick," Dee remarked.

O shrugged. "But it hit Casper's car. And it stopped the game."

"Well, you didn't know. Ian should have told you the rules at the start." She scooped up a handful of sand, still slightly damp with dew, and began sifting through it with her fingers to pick out the cypress needles and cones. "Did you play kickball in New York?"

"I played a little bit." O ran a hand over the sand, smoothing a patch.

"What was New York like? I always hear such scary things. People getting mugged all the time, or murdered. And it's so dirty."

"Oh, it was not so bad. We lived in a nice part of the city." O paused, as if thinking of New York reminded him of something.

"What?"

Dee could see him measuring her, deciding what he could and couldn't say. "Tell me," she added. "You can tell me anything." It was almost a plea, this desire to know him better.

"We lived on the Upper East Side, where most of the apartment buildings have doormen." He smiled at her blank look of suburban ignorance. "They are men who sit at the entrance of the building, like a guard, except they help you too, with packages and shopping and hailing you taxis and things like that. There were not many ... people like us in that neighborhood. So every time I walked past a doorman he would watch me closely, and whistle so the doorman at the next building would notice, and *he* would watch me, and whistle. This whistling would happen all the way down the block. Usually they only did this when a pretty girl walked past. Even once they knew me, and had seen me walk by every day for months, they did this thing with the whistling. They said it was a joke, and maybe after a while it was for them, but it never felt like a joke to me. It was like they were waiting for me to do something."

"Do what?"

"Steal something, or mug someone, or throw a rock."

"That's ..." Dee didn't know what it was. She was still trying to get her head around the idea of him living in an apartment, rather than a house the way she and all her friends did. But she lived in the suburbs. There weren't that many apartments out here. "What about your own doorman?"

"He was all right, eventually. He was teased by some of the other doormen, but my father gave him a generous Christmas tip, and that helped. He would never hail us a taxi, though, not even when we could see empty ones driving by. He would say there were none, or that they were going to other jobs. I only went in two taxis the whole time we lived there."

Dee herself had never been in a taxi—had never needed to. What an exotic life, to need a taxi! "Tell me some more about Ghana," she said, just to hear him talk.

Osei sat up straighter. "What would you like to know about my country?" The mention of Ghana seemed to make him even more formal.

"Well ..." Dee paused, considering whether or not to bring up a thought that had lodged in her head when Ghana had first been mentioned. But she liked him—really liked him—and wanted to be as open with him as she could. "Don't they . . . eat people there?"

O smiled. "You are thinking of Papua New *Guinea*. Not Ghana. Papua New Guinea is near Australia."

"Oh! Sorry."

"That is all right. My sister, Sisi, had a teacher once in Rome who made that mistake too, and assigned her to do a class report on cannibalism. She practiced it on me first, so I heard all about it."

This was even more surprising than the doormen and the taxis. "How do you say 'cannibalism' in Italian?"

"*Cannibalismo*."

Dee giggled, then grew serious. "Maybe you can explain to me why people eat each other, then. I've never understood it. It's just so gross."

"Well, one reason is that sometimes there is not enough food. If there is a famine, or people are stuck somewhere with nothing to eat. Did you hear about the plane crash in the Andes two years ago where people had to eat the dead to survive?"

Dee shuddered, not sure why she had turned the conversation in this direction, but not sure she wanted to change it either. She had never talked about anything this serious with any other boy—or girl, for that matter.

"But most of the time cannibalism is not about hunger," O continued. "People eat others if they have beaten them in battle, as a trophy of war. Or sometimes they eat part of someone they love who has passed. It is like bringing them back into the community—like reincarnating them through their own body."

"Ew!"

O chuckled. "In Ghana we dance and sing after someone has passed, but we do not eat them!"

Dee thought of her grandfather lying in an open coffin in a church in South Carolina. It had been solemn and awkward and her new shoes had pinched. "You dance?"

"Yes. It is a big party that goes on all night, with food and bands playing and many people. The family puts up billboards around town to advertise and everybody comes. We spend a great deal of money on a funeral—as much as we do on a wedding." His accent seemed to become more African as he talked about Ghana, his vowels more extreme and his voice more emphatic.

"Very strange. Do you go to Ghana a lot?"

"We visit every summer to see my grandparents."

"And you like it?"

"Of course."

"When you go there, do you stay in the city or the country?"

"Both. We have a house in Accra and a house in my grandfather's village."

Dee wanted to ask if the house was a mud hut with a grass roof as she'd seen in photos of Africa in her dad's *National Geographic*. But her mistakes over cannibalism and over dashikis earlier had stung her, and she didn't dare ask something else that would reveal more ignorance.

She thought about what she could ask. In the silence she became very aware of them sitting together under the cypress trees, the playground active around them but everyone also angled toward them, watching. She wished they were walking or climbing the jungle gym or swinging on the swings rather than sitting still.

"Are there lots of wild animals there?" Dee could have kicked herself for asking something so obvious, but the conversation seemed in danger of stalling, as it often did when a boy and a girl suddenly felt self-conscious together.

"Yes. We have buffalo, baboons, warthogs, monkeys. And many others."

"Are there elephants?"

"Yes."

Though he seemed willing to be asked questions, he was not asking her anything. But boys rarely did—they were better at talking than at listening, and better at doing than at talking. Dee had not sat and talked with a boy for this long, ever.

Since he didn't ask, Dee could not offer him anything about herself. What would she tell him if he asked? That her parents were very strict. That she liked math but pretended not to. That she was surprised at her own popularity at school given the limitations her mother put on her: she could not go to the mall with her friends, she had never had a birthday party—roller-skating or taking everyone to the movies. That she occasionally felt low for no reason. That Mimi had read her tarot cards recently and said things would soon change drastically for her. Dee had assumed she meant the move to junior high in the fall, but now, watching Osei smoothing and roughing up and smoothing the sand over and over, his hand so dark against the pale surface, she thought maybe "soon" was sooner than she'd expected.

Then he glanced up and smiled at her, his face half-turned so that he looked mischievous, and all of the words said and unsaid, the questions asked and unasked, the awkward silences, were swept away by the warmth that surged through her. Dee had never been like Blanca and a couple other girls, putting themselves forward, pursuing the boys and encouraging them to take an interest. Her clothes were not tight and shiny. She did not push out her growing breasts, but hunched over to downplay them. She had not been experimenting with boys around the corner by the gym doors, and had only kissed when they played spin the bottle during recess—and then only twice, as it was shut down by teachers once they found out what was going on. But her response to O was not experimental. *This is what I have been waiting for*, she thought. *This.*

It made her do what she had wanted to do since first lining up behind him before school: she reached over and touched his head, feeling the fuzz of his hair follow the curve of his perfect skull.

Osei did not pull back, nor did his smile disappear. He reached over in turn and laid his hand along her cheek. Dee turned her face to lean into it, like a cat being petted.

"You have a beautiful head," she said.

"And you, a beautiful face."

Surprise and relief flooded through her. He felt the same as she did; they could relax into each other. Dee understood now that real couples didn't have to ask each other to go together: they already *were* together.

Asking was babyish, a joke for children. She and Osei had already gone way beyond that.

They remained in their pose, like a modern sculpture of lovers, all heads and smiles and arms extended and interconnected, the outside world excluded. Dee heard Mimi nearby hiss, "Dee, what are you *doing*?" In the distance, Blanca began to chant:

> O and Dee, sittin' in a tree
> K-I-S-S-I-N-G
> First comes love, then comes marriage
> Then comes Dee with a baby carriage!

As a whistle was blown they continued to touch each other. Teachers on playground duty blew their whistle when anyone was doing something they shouldn't: pushing another student, hanging upside down from the monkey bars, throwing sand, climbing the fence. Whenever the whistle sounded, students halted and looked around to see who would get in trouble.

O wouldn't know about that, but he must have guessed what it meant, for as Mr. Brabant strode toward them, still blowing his whistle, he dropped his hand from Dee's burning cheek. Dazed, she left her hand on his head for a moment longer.

"Stop that! Get up this minute, you two." His voice was like a whip cracking. O scrambled to his feet. Though Dee felt resistance welling, it was too awkward to continue sitting on the sand with everyone gathering around and staring down at her. She took her time getting up, though, brushing sand from her jeans, not meeting Mr. Brabant's fury.

"You are *not* to touch other students inappropriately. Maybe things are different where you come from and you don't know any better," he directed at O, "but at this school boys and girls don't touch each other like that." The touching seemed to disturb him far more than any of the kissing he had caught the sixth graders doing all year. Maybe he sensed it was more meaningful, more heartfelt, more intimate—too intimate for a school playground. He turned to Dee. "And I'm surprised at you, Dee. You should know better. Now go inside and hand out the math worksheets."

Dee had never been suspended or had a detention or been disciplined in any way at school, for she had not needed it. And she was getting off lightly: any other student would have been sent to the principal's office for a scolding, and possibly a phone call to their parents. Instead she was being given a task she would have willingly done anyway. It seemed Mr. Brabant couldn't bring himself to punish his favorite student too harshly.

Another time his words and tone would have stung, for of all the adults at school, Mr. Brabant was the one she most wanted to please. But today was different—Dee had found someone new whose opinion she suddenly cared about more. And someone Mr. Brabant was judging. Dee didn't like his tone. Still, she could not disobey her teacher. The best response, she decided, was to take her time rather than rush to please him. As she began to saunter past Mr. Brabant toward the entrance, she could feel him staring at her, clearly aghast at her new attitude. It made Dee feel powerful.

✻

They waited for Mr. Brabant to punish the new boy the way he needed to be punished. Ian could have shown him what to do: a good old-fashioned crack with a ruler on the black hand that had dared to touch Dee's cheek. The moment he'd seen them with their arms around each other, a rage had coursed through Ian that he was still finding hard to control. Yet Mr. Brabant simply looked lost—and old, the bags under his eyes more pronounced. His teacher's pet had finally rebelled and he didn't know what to do about it.

Ian coughed to break the spell. Somebody had to. Mr. Brabant shook his head, then made a clear effort to pull himself together. Fixing his eyes on O, he stuck out his jaw. "Watch yourself, boy," he said.

O looked back at the teacher and said nothing. The pause between them seemed to last an eternity, broken only by Miss Lode appearing, breathless. "Is everything all right?" she asked, her voice high with nerves.

"It better be," Mr. Brabant barked. "It will be, when a certain boy here understands the rules of this school. Right, Osei?"

"Yes, sir."

"Osei, here we don't use 'sir' and 'ma'am,'" Miss Lode interjected, her tone gentle compared to her colleague's. "We call teachers by their names. You should call him Mr. Brabant and me Miss Lode."

"Yes, Miss Lode."

"I can handle him, Diane."

"Of course. I didn't mean to—" She was saved by the bell ringing.

"All right—go and line up." Mr. Brabant raised his voice to include all the students surrounding him.

O moved, but slowly—much as Dee had just done—to make clear he was not really following an order, but happening to go in the right direction.

"Did I miss something?" Miss Lode said in a low voice.

"Inappropriate behavior," Mr. Brabant muttered. "He was touching Dee. Typical."

Miss Lode looked puzzled. "Gosh. Have you—have you been around many . . . black people?"

"A whole platoon."

"Oh, I—sorry, I didn't mean to ask about that . . . time."

"Seeing his hand on her made me sick."

Miss Lode caught sight of Ian listening and nudged Mr. Brabant. "Right, Ian, go and get in line," he commanded.

"I will, Mr. Brabant—as soon as I collect the ball."

Mr. Brabant grunted, and strode toward the lines forming, Miss Lode following in his wake.

Midway across the playground, Mimi had fallen into step beside O. Ian watched as they walked together, talking. At one point O leaned toward Ian's girlfriend as if to listen to her more closely; then he nodded, said something, and Mimi laughed.

Ian frowned.

"That bastard, touching her. Made me feel sick too." Rod was at Ian's side, holding the kickball.

Ian stared at his girlfriend. "I didn't see that. Did he just touch her?"

"Not Mimi. *Dee.* He was touching Dee under the trees. And *she* was touching *him.*" Rod was working himself into a rage, his cheeks bright red.

"He touches all the girls," Ian muttered. "He'll be going all the way with them soon. That's how boys like him are. Unless we stop him."

"Yeah." Rod bounced the kickball a couple times, as if it were a basketball. "How are we gonna do that?"

"We have to turn her against him." Ian thought for a moment. "No, that's too obvious—Dee won't fall for that, she's too smart. Maybe ... him against her. Yeah, that might be better. And more fun."

"What? You're not gonna hurt Dee, are you? 'Cause that's not fair. I just want a chance with her, that's all."

"I'm not going to hurt her, I'm just going to ... break them up."

"Good. But, Ian ..."

"What?"

"Why didn't you pick me for your team during kickball?"

Ian sighed inwardly. He was going to have to shake off Rod. He'd planned to do so when they moved on to junior high—changing schools always caused a reshuffling among friends. But he wasn't sure he could wait that long. Rod was beginning to demand more and more; he was too much effort for the little he delivered.

"I had to give the new boy a chance," Ian explained. "Now I wish I hadn't, especially since he stopped the game with that kick."

"But you could've chosen me as well as him."

"Yeah, but then the team might have been too lop-sided. I mean, you're a good player, of course. Anybody could see that from your kick—and you scored the only run for your team, right?"

Rod beamed.

"If the black boy was good too, our team would have been *too* good with you and him on it, and the game no fun. I was just balancing it out."

Rod frowned, puzzled by the backhandedness of the compliment, though enjoying the praise too.

"Go and get in line," Ian ordered. "I'll be there in a minute."

Rod nodded, then bounced the ball again, held it in front of him, and drop-kicked it away toward the lines of students. He raced off after it, as forgetful and happy as a dog. If only it were that easy, Ian thought. He did not move, remaining under the trees, watching the students go toward their teachers. He needed some space to think.

The moment the black boy walked onto the playground that morning, Ian had felt something shift. It was what an earthquake must feel like, the ground being rearranged and becoming unreliable. The students had had almost the whole year—indeed, the past seven years at elementary school—to get into their established groups, with their hierarchies of leaders and followers. It ran smoothly—until one boy arrived to destabilize everything. One massive kick of a ball, one touch of a girl's cheek, and the order had changed. He scrutinized O, now in his line, and could see the rearrangement going on to include this new leader—the shifts as other students subtly turned toward him, as if he were a light they followed, like plants seeking the sun. As Ian watched, Casper stepped up behind O and began talking to him. He gestured over the fence, clearly discussing O's kick, and they nodded. Just like that, the black boy had gained the respect of the most popular boy in school, was going with the most popular girl, and had laughed with Ian's girlfriend—and it wasn't even lunchtime yet.

"Popular" was not a word that would ever be attached to Ian. No one chatted and laughed with him. They hadn't for a long time. He wasn't sure exactly how it happened, but he had become the boy they feared but didn't respect. He hadn't planned it that way, but when he'd started fourth grade and moved up to the older-class playground, his brother had gone on to junior high and Ian found himself inheriting a position of power that few questioned. It came with perks: lunch money handed over, a place by the gym door away from the teachers whenever he wanted it, automatic captaincy of kickball and softball teams, and Rod, his assistant and defender—though Ian could have done without a buffoon as his right-hand man.

The whistle blew and Ian looked up, knowing it was for him. The lines were disappearing inside and Miss Lode was waving at him to come in. Even the teachers feared Ian a little; she would not punish him for hanging back, though later she would probably complain about him in the teachers' lounge. Once he had hung outside the door and heard one teacher say to another, "Ian *is* the last of the Murphys, right? There isn't some sister sneaking up from behind? I don't think I could take another, after him and his brothers. I've paid my dues with that family."

"Oh, his wings will be clipped in junior high," the other had replied. "Little fish in a big pond and all that." The two had chuckled. For that laugh, Ian had keyed both of their cars.

As far as he could tell, his brothers were still big fish. The brother above him was smoking now, and said he had gone all the way with his girlfriend.

Before he started toward the school doors at the end of his class line, Ian had to make a conscious effort to unclench his jaw and his fists.

As he passed the door to Mr. Brabant's classroom, he glanced inside. O was sitting at his desk, looking down at a sheet of paper. Standing behind him, Dee was handing a sheet to Casper, who was smiling at her with his natural privilege. An outsider seeing them together could have mistaken them for boyfriend and girlfriend. And the black boy wasn't seeing any of this.

Ian smirked as he hurried to catch up with his classmates. He knew now what he would do.

At the water fountain next to Miss Lode's classroom, a fourth grader was bending over to drink. It would be so easy to nudge her into the spigot and bloody her lip; Ian had done so with other students many times before. Today, however, the plan forming in his head made him feel magnanimous, and he passed the girl without touching her. She flinched anyway.

PART III

LUNCH

One day when I was walking
A-walking to the fair
I met a señorita
With flowers in her hair

Oh, shake it, señorita
Shake it if you can
Shake it like a milkshake
And shake it once again

Oh, she waddles to the bottom
She waddles to the top
She turns around and turns around
Until she has to stop!

By the time the bell rang for lunch, the tension lurking all morning had taken over. During Spelling Mimi's head had begun to throb, and flashing lights that originated in the corners of her eyes gradually spread across her vision. As the class was finishing its lesson on irregular silent letters, she could barely see the blackboard to copy down the words they had to learn for homework, which Miss Lode had chosen specifically from Shakespeare to tie in with other lessons:

abhor	monkey
gnaw	subtle
chaos	sword
honest	tongue
knave	wretch

"Miss Lode's in a funny mood, choosing these words," Jennifer muttered next to her. "They're not even very hard! And we never use some of them. What does 'knave' mean, anyway?"

"A naughty boy," Mimi replied. She and Dee had

watched *Romeo and Juliet* on TV a few weeks before and heard the word then. Mimi had fallen hard for Romeo.

"Who did she say Shakespeare is?"

"You know! He wrote *A Midsummer Night's Dream*." The two sixth grade classes were putting on a version of the play at the end of the year. Mimi was playing a fairy. She shook her head, though she knew it wouldn't clear her vision. "Can you read the words to me?"

Jennifer looked sympathetic. "Head hurt again?"

"Yes." Mimi didn't tell many friends about the headaches she'd begun having in the past six months, as she didn't want to be fussed over, but it was hard to hide them from Jennifer, who sat next to her and seemed attuned to her pain. Jennifer covered for her, particularly when Mimi had to rush from the classroom. "Period," she'd whisper to Miss Lode, who would nod nervously. Menstruation was a solemn topic in sixth grade, though many of the girls were still waiting for it to happen. Those who could took advantage of the teachers' embarrassment about it. But Jennifer's lie was closer to the truth than she knew, for Mimi had begun having headaches around the time her period started. Her mother told her it was a sign of growing up, but Mimi wasn't reassured.

She didn't have to rush out today, gauging that she could make it to lunch. Copying the spelling list under Jennifer's tutelage, she ignored the squeezing on her head and the diamonds of light dancing in front of her eyes, until at last the lunch bell rang. Even then Mimi did not run off, but filed out with the others. She was about to head to the girls' bathroom in the basement when a hand gripped her arm. Ian. Immediately she felt worse, urgently so.

"Hang on a minute," he said. "Anyone would think you're avoiding me. You're not, are you?" He wore a complicated look: smiling as if he were joking, yet Mimi knew he was not. Behind the smile was an unyielding, rock-hard layer.

"No," she said. "I just have a headache." She tried to smile back, but her nausea was rising rapidly. "I have to go to—"

"I need you to do something for me."

"What?"

"Has Casper ever given Dee anything? Notes or jewelry or anything?"

"I—I don't know. Maybe. But it's never been like that between them, really." Mimi couldn't think about anything except getting to the bathroom.

"Find out, and whatever it is, get it for me."

"All right. I really need to go . . ." Mimi pulled away from Ian and hurried down the stairs to the girls' bathroom. Running into a stall, she dropped to her knees and threw up into the toilet. Afterward she flushed, then sat back on her heels, leaned against the divider, and closed her eyes. Mercifully no one was there to ask if she was all right or to go and get a teacher.

It was remarkable how being sick cleared not just her stomach: the flashing diamonds had vanished, and her head no longer hurt. The bathroom was quiet except for the slow filling of the cistern. It stank of disinfectant, and of the coarse brown paper towels you never found anywhere other than in school bathrooms.

Its walls were painted battleship gray and, combined with the fluorescent lights, made everyone look ugly and ill, even Blanca and Dee. Despite the light and the smell, girls liked to hang out down here: it was one of the few places where teachers rarely came unless on patrol, for they had their own toilet next to the teachers' lounge.

What Mimi really wanted to do now was to lie down and press her cheek against the cool tiled floor and think about nothing, simply let the river of the day wash over her.

But she could not do that. The floor smelled too strongly of bleach, and besides, someone was bound to come in, and Mimi's friends were expecting her at the cafeteria and would notice if she didn't appear soon. She rinsed out her mouth and splashed water on her cheeks, then peered at herself in the mirror. She looked awful. Pulling out a lipstick she had stolen from her older sister, Mimi dotted some on her cheeks and rubbed it in. Girls were not allowed to wear makeup at school, but she hoped no one would notice. She took one last look at herself, tried to smile, then said aloud, "Give him what he wants—then he'll let you go." That would be her strategy.

Mimi was surprised to see Dee and Osei together outside the cafeteria, their heads bent over something, foreheads touching. Dee was one of a handful of children who went home for lunch, as she lived close by. Her mother would be expecting her back on time. Over the years Mimi had gone home with her after school a few times to play, and noted Dee's mother's thin mouth that never smiled, the pointed looks at her watch, the lack of a snack, the liver served for dinner, the heightened tension when the father arrived home and frowned at discovering an unexpected guest. It made her appreciate her own parents more. Gradually she and Dee gravitated to Mimi's house, where her mother gave them plates of Oreos and let them watch TV.

Now Dee glanced at the clock in the hall, pushed something into a pencil case—the pink one she had described to Mimi earlier—and stuffed it in her backpack. She spoke to O, looked around, then kissed him briefly before running off. Mimi should have been shocked by the kiss, especially since they would've gotten into trouble if a teacher had seen them; but after their flagrant touching on the playground it seemed anticlimactic. Mimi could still picture their arms, black and white, reaching for each other. It was the sexiest thing she'd ever seen, even more powerful than Romeo and Juliet making out during the balcony scene.

As Dee ran, the pink case fell from her open backpack, which she had been in too much of a hurry to zip shut. Mimi called out, but her friend was gone. O had already walked away toward the cafeteria, so she went over to pick it up. Running her fingers over the embossed strawberries, she thought the case was indeed sweet, as Dee had said, though it was not to Mimi's taste. She would give it back after lunch. Tucking it into her own backpack, she headed for the cafeteria.

Blanca waved at her from a table and pointed to the seat she was saving—not easy in the crowded room.

"Where've you been?" she shouted. "Everybody wants this seat!"

"I'll be right there," Mimi called back. "Anything you want?"

"More tater tots!"

Blanca loved food, as she loved any sort of sensory experience, and Mimi often passed French fries, or cherries from fruit cocktail, or cartons of chocolate milk on to her. Now, although empty, her stomach was sore and all she wanted was Kool-Aid. However, she forced herself to take a tray, where the lunch ladies would serve up Salisbury steak and tater tots and a quivering slice of lemon meringue pie. Blanca and the others would happily eat anything Mimi didn't want.

As she waited in line she watched O, one student ahead of her. The lunch ladies were all black too, and Mimi thought they might smile a special smile at him, as a signal that he was one of them. Instead, when she saw him, the lady serving the Salisbury steak froze, her spoon suspended, the tomato sauce dripping down the gristly piece of meat and onto O's tray. The lady next to her chuckled. "C'mon, Jeanette, give the boy his steak!" she said as she gave O two spoonfuls of tater tots.

When he had moved on, Mimi heard the Salisbury steak lady say to the others, "That poor boy."

"What do you mean, 'poor boy'?" the tater tots lady demanded. "This is a good school. He's lucky to go here."

"Don't tell me you don't know what I mean. Do you want your son walking onto a playground where he's different from everybody else?"

"If he's gonna get a good education, sure. 'Sides, he's

a new boy. New boys always have it hard at first. He'll get used to it."

"Are you a fool or what? It's not him who has to get used to it. It's white people got to get used to it! And do you think they will? They'll give him hell out there—and in the classroom too, I bet. Teachers are as bad as the kids. Worse, 'cause they oughta know better."

Mimi stood still with her tray, listening. Although she had been served by the lunch ladies for years, she had rarely heard them say anything other than "one scoop or two?" when doling out mashed potatoes. Certainly they had never said anything about one of the students; and nothing like this.

The lady serving tater tots suddenly became aware of Mimi and nudged the other two. "You want tater tots, honey? We got extra here." She gave her three spoonfuls before Mimi could say anything. "Denise, go on and give her a big slice of pie. The biggest. She's looking peaky."

Mimi could not stop them from heaping her tray with far too much food. "There," the tater tots lady said. "You all right now? You got everything you need?" She held Mimi's eyes for a beat longer than necessary.

Mimi nodded and pulled away, confused.

Ahead of her, Osei was motionless with his tray, looking around at the full tables. Mimi wondered if he'd heard any of what the lunch ladies had said. She felt sorry for him, standing there wondering where to sit. At least no one was staring at him, and the room didn't go silent as the playground had before school. Students were always louder when there was food.

For a moment she considered asking him to sit with her and Blanca and the others; they could squeeze him in if the girls crowded together. She suspected that Dee would do that if she were here. But Mimi wouldn't: she was more pragmatic than Dee. It was an unwritten rule that boys and girls didn't sit together in the cafeteria; it would cause almost as much uproar as his skin color.

At one table she saw Ian start to get to his feet, but then, closer to O, Casper gestured him over and made someone next to him move and give the new boy his seat. O slid into place and was suddenly locked in with all the other boys like a chess piece on a board. Ian remained half-standing, his eyes shifting from side to side to see if anyone had noticed that he'd been cut off, like when someone speaks but others don't hear them and carry on their conversation, leaving the speaker hanging. The boys with Ian must have had a sixth sense around him and were carefully engaged in eating or joking or looking the other way. Only Mimi was caught with her eyes on him. He glared at her, and she turned away to hurry to her seat.

"Ooh, you got lucky," Blanca cooed, popping a tater tot in her mouth. "Look how many you got! You gonna eat that pie?"

Mimi shook her head and pushed the tray into the middle of the table, holding back only a cup of Kool-Aid. Blanca and the others fell on the extra food, even the tough steak. It made her feel ill to watch, and she was afraid to look up and see Ian again, so she kept her eyes on her backpack under the table. Inside was Dee's strawberry pencil case. It wasn't zipped shut, and there was a scrap of paper sticking out of the gap. Mimi knew she should leave it; it wasn't hers to read. But she couldn't help it: seeing Dee and O with their heads touching over the case made her want a little bit of whatever it was they had, even if it meant looking through her friend's things. Mimi glanced up: the girls across from her were arguing over how to divide up the lemon meringue pie. She pulled out the piece of paper.

There was a name and address and phone number written on it:

Osei Kokote
4501 Nicosia Boulevard, Apt. 511
652-3970

She thought for a moment. This was the suburbs; most people lived in houses. Mimi knew only one girl who lived in an apartment rather than a house, and that was a girl with a single mother, whose father had left when she was little. Her apartment had been on the poorer side of town. But Nicosia Boulevard was a big road, with offices and fancy stores and new apartment buildings that had marble entrances and valet parking like at hotels. She had heard some of the apartments even had elevators that opened straight into the rooms. If they lived there, O's family wasn't poor like the girl with the single mother; clearly they were rich.

She could only imagine Dee had the address written down so that they could meet outside of school. They would never go to Dee's house—her mother would kill her for meeting any boy, much less a black one. O's family must not be so concerned. Mimi would have to get ready with an alibi for her—the first of many, she expected. She sighed.

"We're gonna go jump Double Dutch," Blanca announced, standing and stretching, her pink top riding up so that her midriff showed—a display that was not an accident. "You coming?"

"Yeah." Mimi stuffed the slip of paper back in the pencil case, then hesitated over whether or not to zip it shut. Would Dee notice it had been changed? She'd better leave it.

"What are you doing?" For once Blanca was taking an interest in someone else.

"Nothing—I just spilled juice in my lap." Mimi rubbed vigorously at her bag, at the same time pushing the pencil case deep inside.

"Come on!" Blanca ran over to the table where Casper was sitting with other boys, put her hands on his shoulders, and rested her chin on his head so that her long curls tumbled over his face. "Casss-perrr," she sang, drawing out the syllables, "are you coming?"

"Um." Casper pushed her hair aside, looking embarrassed. "Where am I going, Blanca?"

"Don't you remember? You promised to watch me jump Double Dutch!"

"I did?"

"Casper!" Blanca straightened up and swatted his arm. "You told me you would this morning! You'll get to see me dance." She began to sing, snapping her fingers in time as she pretended to jump Double Dutch to invisible ropes:

One day when I was walking
A-walking to the fair
I met a señorita
With flowers in her hair

"Oh Lord," Mimi murmured. She caught Osei's eye; he was trying not to laugh. "Blanca, stop it!"

But Blanca didn't stop. Turning her back to Casper and pouting over her shoulder, she began to swish her hips back and forth as she jumped:

Oh, shake it, señorita
Shake it if you can
Shake it like a milkshake
And shake it once again

"OK, OK!" Casper protested. Getting to his feet and saving them all from even more embarrassment, he allowed Blanca to pull him away. He was smiling, though. Whatever it was about Blanca that appealed to him—her spirited energy, her attention, her blossoming sexiness—he was into her.

As she followed the couple, Mimi could feel Ian's presence at the next table, his eyes seeming to bore into her head to penetrate her thoughts. The feeling made her hurry to get out to the playground.

✻

One of the hardest moments in a new student's day is finding a place to eat in the cafeteria. It's rushed and chaotic, and there are no assigned seats, so everyone sits with their friends. But a new student doesn't have friends yet, so there is nowhere obvious to sit. Osei had been through this before, and knew there were two ways to do it. You could go in first and sit at an empty table and let them come to you. That way you didn't make the mistake of sitting with potential enemies, or of trying too hard to push yourself onto a group. They got to choose you, which they preferred. On the other hand, there was also the risk that no one would sit with you, that you'd end up alone, a ring of empty seats around you like a no-man's-land surrounding a radioactive dump.

Or you could hold back, stand at the end of the line so people were already sitting and you chose where to slot yourself in. If it was crowded there were usually only a couple places left, and the people sitting there didn't have the option to get up and move and leave you stranded. But a lot of times the only vacant seats were with the unpopular kids: the weak, the stupid, the smelly, or those who are disliked for some mysterious reason that no one understands. It wasn't a great idea to start out your school life sitting with them, because whatever it was that was stuck on them got stuck on you too.

Osei had tried both options, and usually went for the second. He preferred to have some control over what happened, or at least be able to predict it. If he was going to end up with the outcasts, he could at least choose his fate.

Today he didn't have much choice anyway, as Dee had held him back to get his address and phone number so that she could call him about doing something, and maybe come over after school one day. She hadn't offered hers, he noticed. He didn't ask why he couldn't go to her house, because he knew why: he was not a parent pleaser. His experiences going home with other boys to play had not been successes. There was the shock at his skin color, the silence, and then the over-politeness from the parents. O was never asked to stay for supper.

He and Dee had remained behind, talking, until she saw the time and cried, "Mom'll kill me for being so late!"

His own mother would chide him for being late but not much more; she saved her shouts and tears for more important things. But Dee's mother seemed to have a hold on her. Grabbing her bag, she had been about to race off, but then looked around and kissed him before hurrying away. Though brief, the gesture made him grin. He couldn't believe his luck that a girl like Dee wanted to kiss him.

The moment she disappeared, the world flattened and darkened. Dee had made Osei's morning bearable. More than that, she had given it color. Now, without her, things shifted back to black and white.

Osei had been friends with girls before. Not in America, but in Ghana: when he visited each summer there were girls in his grandfather's village he'd played with since he was little. It was easy with them—he didn't feel like an outsider, or have to explain things, or not say things. They shared a familiarity, similar to how he was with his sister, Sisi, that made it easy to be together.

He had even gone further with girls, at school in New

York. There was a time earlier that year when every-body began experimenting in the playground, when boys and girls got together at lunchtime and broke up by the end of the day. They never did much. It was like tagging someone and then running away. Sometimes they held hands, or kissed, fast and sloppy. One boy touched a girl's chest, even though there was not much there, and got slapped and suspended. It was talked about for weeks.

O was amazed that he got attention from any girls at all, since he was barely tolerated by anyone. But one day when it seemed everyone was pairing off—like a flu that had descended on the playground and infected all the students—a girl named Toni came up to him and said, "Do you like me?" She had never spoken to him before.

"You're all right," he said, trying to sound ca-sual and American. She looked so disappointed and embarrassed—a combination O recognized could be potentially dangerous—that he forced himself to look at her more carefully. She was wearing plaid bell bottoms and a green turtleneck sweater tight enough that he could see the outline of her new bust. "I like your sweater," he added, and she smiled and looked so expectant that he knew he was supposed to say more. And he knew what he had to say, for he'd heard others use the words many times that week. "Will you go with me?" he asked.

Toni looked around, as if for support from her friends. They were off to the side, whispering and laughing, and O almost said, "Never mind, please forget that I asked you." But then she said yes, and so he went with her, which involved standing around together while others pointed and giggled. "Do you have any brothers or sisters?" he tried asking finally, just to be polite. But that made Toni giggle too, and Osei got fed up and walked away. "I'm breaking up with you!" she shouted after him. "You're dumped!"

O almost gave her the finger, but the thought of what his mother would say if she saw the rude American gesture, especially using it at a girl, stopped him.

With the next girl—Pam—he got a little further. He found out that she had two sisters and that her favorite color was yellow. They walked around the playground and even held hands. When he went to kiss her, though, she pushed him away. "You smell," she said. "I knew you would."

"Fine," Osei answered. "I didn't want to go with you anyway." It seemed important to get that in first, to be the dumper rather than the one getting dumped.

Pam ran to her friends at the far end of the playground, where shrieks of indignation flew up from the other girls, making them sound like a flock of angry seagulls. They stayed away from him as if he were toxic for the rest of the months Osei was at that school, glaring at him every chance they got, and making a show of talking about him and laughing. Whenever he joined a line they ostentatiously moved away from him. Girls could be a lot meaner than boys, and hold on to grudges for longer, rather than fight them out of their systems the way boys did. Their treatment of him was harder to cope with than he'd expected, and for that reason alone it was a relief to move to Washington to change schools and get away from them.

Toni and Pam felt like rehearsals for a play he would be in later, with other people—a read-through of lines without any feeling behind them, except for the occasional jolt of pleasure from physical contact, or even just the thought of it.

With Dee it was completely different: a seductive blend of physical attraction, curiosity, and acceptance that he had never had from anyone before. She asked him a lot of questions, and really listened to the answers, her maple-syrup eyes unwavering on his, nodding and leaning toward him. Dee would never giggle with her friends at him, or say he smelled, or stare at him in a funny way. She managed to balance curiosity about the things that made O different from her with an acceptance of him that was flattering and made him want to put his arms around her and hold her, feeling the warmth of her body and blotting out the rest of the school, the rest of the world.

Now, without her, he stood with a tray full of congealed food he would have to force himself to eat, served to him by lunch ladies who he suspected were talking about him behind his back, and looked out over the noisy tables full of students shouting and laughing, blowing through straws to make bubbles in their milk cartons, throwing tater tots in the air and trying to catch them in their mouths. It was hot and noisy and smelled meaty, and there were no seats free except at the table reserved for the losers. There were three of them. One had been the weak player on Osei's team during kickball and looked like he might be the source of the meaty smell, one had squinty eyes, and the third seemed permanently sad. They were staring fearfully at O. They might have been scared of a black boy sitting with them, but he had a feeling it was not just that. No, they were scared of a *successful* boy sitting with them. A boy who had kicked a ball farther than they could ever dream of doing. A boy who was going with Dee and was now being offered two places to sit, and not with them. O saw the relief in their eyes as Casper waved him over, nodding at the boy next to him to move. At the same time, Ian was getting to his feet. O was going to have to choose between them.

There was no choice, really. Is there ever between the darkness and the light? You walk toward the smile rather than the frown. O pretended not to see Ian, nodded at Casper, and went over to sit down by him. Even as he did it he knew he had made a tricky choice that could backfire. Ian was the kind of boy who didn't like to be ignored or rejected.

"Hey," Casper said.

"Hey," O repeated, conscious that he should imitate to fit in. In New York people said "Hi"; here they said "Hey." He hunched over his food, picked up a fork and pushed the grim steak around in its sauce, thinking of the can of Coke and the sandwich his mother had made for him and that he'd left in his desk. He resorted to a tater tot. They at least nominally resembled what they were supposed to be, though Osei thought of his mother's roast potatoes and sighed.

"It's pretty terrible," Casper said with a chuckle. "The only day the food's any good is Friday when they serve pizza."

There was a Casper in every school, popular enough

that he could afford to be genuinely nice to people. He was probably nice even to the three losers at the other table, because he could be. Casper had entitlement. Osei's father liked to say it was always better to befriend a man whose family has been wealthy for generations than a poor man who has worked his way up and will be nasty to those who remain where he has come from. The latter would be Ian.

"I am very sorry about your parents' car," he said, to get that out of the way.

Casper looked puzzled. "What about it?"

"I hit it with my kick earlier."

"Oh." Casper waved a hand. "No big deal."

"But the roof might be dented."

"Nah. Oldsmobiles are indestructible."

For a while Casper and the boys around him talked among themselves and Osei was able to eat peacefully. Then, during a lull, Casper threw out a question to draw him in naturally to the group. "When you lived in New York, were you a Jets or a Giants fan?"

Osei didn't have to think about that one. "Giants," he answered immediately. "I will never support a team whose quarterback wears pantyhose!"

The table exploded. The Jets' quarterback, Joe Namath, had recently worn pantyhose in a commercial, and every boy at the table had something to say about it.

"Faggot!"

"I saw that commercial with my *mother* in the room. I was so embarrassed!"

"He must've been paid a whole lot of money to do that."

"He shaved his legs for that commercial! You can see

his legs are smooth, and not from the pantyhose. He *shaved!*"

"You wouldn't catch me doing that to my legs, not for any amount of money."

"Faggot!"

"No he's not—a girl kisses him at the end."

"He's still a faggot!"

In the midst of it all, Casper grinned at O. "Besides, Namath threw too many interceptions," he said. "Give me Sonny Jurgensen any day. Even old and on a bad day, he throws better than Namath."

Osei nodded, though he wasn't sure who Sonny Jurgensen was. He must be a Washington Redskins quarterback. O would have to find out more about them if he wanted to get along with these boys. Himself, he preferred baseball, but there was no team in this city.

He was saved from having to reveal his ignorance of the local football team by a group of girls coming over to the table. The loudest of them insisted on Casper coming to watch her jump rope, shamelessly dancing in a way that was funny and embarrassing at the same time. Among the girls was Dee's friend Mimi, whom Osei had spoken to during morning recess and who seemed friendly. Her cheeks were flushed, as if smeared with something, and her braces glinted. Her bright red hair would have been much remarked upon in his grandfather's village. White skin was a surprise anyway, but coupled with red hair—well, that was devilish. "C'mon, Blanca," she said softly, pulling on the loud girl's arm. "We'll lose our turn with the rope." She glanced at O and grimaced, which made him smile at her.

"Blame Casper," Blanca retorted. "He's the one who's taking so long!"

Casper sighed in exaggerated exasperation and shrugged at Osei as Blanca pulled him away.

He hadn't invited Osei to join him, probably thinking he was doing him a favor: what boy would willingly watch a group of girls jump rope? However, the moment he was gone, the atmosphere changed. With Casper as his guardian Osei had been safe, and had started to relax, maybe too much. The boys left were sporty and popular enough to hang out with Casper, but not confident without him. It felt to Osei as if those sitting with him at the table all moved an inch away, literally and figuratively, so that once again he was the outsider. Jokes about Joe Namath had not been enough to save him. Now he had to put his guard back up.

Duncan, the boy who sat across from him in class, was studying him again. When Osei looked straight at him, his eyes slid away. "Can I ask you something?" he said.

"That depends what you ask."

"How do you wash hair like that?"

It was the sort of question O knew well. White people liked to ask a lot about hair care. Also, did black people ever get tanned or sunburned? Were they naturally better at sports and if so, why? Were they better dancers? Did they have better rhythm? Why didn't black people have wrinkles? Back before his mother made him get a haircut and he had a decent Afro, sometimes when Osei was standing in line, the girls behind him would reach out and touch his hair in wonder, then wipe their fingers on their skirts. He couldn't turn around and do the same to them or they would have shrieked and he'd get in trouble. He would have liked to touch their hair—a white girl's silky-smooth long hair was a novelty every bit as curious as his bushy Afro was to them. He'd briefly touched Pam's hair before he'd broken up with her, but running his hand over Dee's head during recess was the first time he'd touched a white girl's hair properly. Even then, hers was in braids, so he hadn't had the true experience. When she came back from lunch he was going to ask her to take it out of the braids so he could feel it loose and get his fingers tangled in it.

"Hey, did you hear what I said?"

"What?" Distracted by thoughts of Dee's hair, O had forgotten to answer Duncan's question. "Oh. I just use a shampoo that has coconut oil in it."

Duncan wrinkled his nose as if at a bad smell. "Oil. Doesn't that make it greasy?"

"Not really."

Duncan looked unconvinced. Osei stood; he would rather be out on the playground than trapped in his seat, trying to explain African hair care to a white boy.

For a second he thought of telling Sisi about it after school and laughing over how the same questions about hair got asked whether you were in London or Rome or Washington. But then he remembered: Sisi wouldn't be home for him to talk to.

She had been devastated when their father was posted to Washington, and had begged her parents to let her live at a friend's house in New York until the end of the school year. Sisi was growing cleverer at getting what she wanted: she didn't ask right away to be allowed to remain in New York for two more years to finish high school. Osei knew that was what she was plotting, though, as he listened on the extension, holding his breath so she wouldn't hear him as she talked about her plans with her friends. "Black is *beautiful*," she always signed off by saying.

Sisi was so persuasive that their parents agreed to her staying with a friend's family in New York for the remainder of the school year while the Kokotes went on ahead to Washington. Osei wanted to tell his parents what he knew about her activities, but had decided to speak to her first. One night, just before the family was due to move, he came and sat on the end of her bed and watched Sisi in front of her dressing table, tying a silk scarf around her hair and applying cocoa butter to her face and arms. He had come to her room with the intention of begging her to move to Washington after all. "You can make friends with people there who take African names and wear African clothes and talk about black liberation," he was going to assure her. What he was thinking was: *Don't leave me alone with our parents. What if I need someone to talk to? Aren't I as important as pan-Africanism or Black Power?* He was all ready to speak—had even opened his mouth—when Sisi gazed at him in the mirror with amusement and said, "What is it, little brother? Have you come to borrow a toy, perhaps? You can have all of them," gesturing at a shelf full of redundant dolls and board games.

"Forget it," he muttered, and stalked out, ignoring her calling after him, "Wait, Osei. What is it?" When she tapped on his bedroom door, he shouted, "Go away!" and turned up his radio. It was easier to be angry at her condescension than to tell her what he really thought. Now he wished he had opened the door, or at least said something to his parents about what she was up to.

In DC he missed her terribly, even in her new radical persona, especially now that she was only a dot at the end of a phone line. The night before his first day of school they'd talked briefly on the phone, but Sisi had said little of consequence and had called him "little brother" again. "I'll be taller than you some day," he'd interrupted. She ignored him, and asked stupid questions about the new apartment. He noticed she asked nothing about her bedroom. He knew now he would not be able to share with her whatever happened to him in his new school—what other kids said and did to him, the everyday moments that constantly reminded him he was different from them and which all added up to a growing feeling of alienation.

Osei had ended the call abruptly, blurting out, "*Black* is beautiful, or so you say," deliberately emphasizing it differently from her. He'd slammed down the phone on Sisi's squawk.

Was black beautiful? He did not even want to have to think about such questions. He just wanted to play ball games, laugh about Joe Namath, touch Dee's hair and smell Herbal Essence shampoo on it.

As Osei left the cafeteria, Ian fell into step beside him, which was kind of a relief, as it was always easier to walk onto a playground with someone at your side rather than alone—even if it was a boy like Ian. O could even forgive Ian's earlier remark about black people being better athletes; he'd heard much worse. He wasn't sure if Ian forgave *him* for choosing to sit with Casper, however.

It appeared he did. "Hey," was all he said.

"Hey," O returned warily.

They wandered the playground together, a boy named Rod trailing behind them until Ian waved him away. Fourth graders were playing kickball. Some fifth graders were arm wrestling on the pirate ship. The girls were playing hopscotch and jumping Double Dutch. Blanca was leaning against Casper, who was tolerating it with grace. Everywhere O went with Ian he noticed other students dropping their eyes as they approached; it was like not wanting to make eye contact with an unpredictable dog—who might be friendly but might just as easily bite you. As they passed, some of the students gave Osei strange looks. Walking around with Ian felt a little like being inducted into a gang he was not sure he wanted to join—or that even wanted him as a member. He wondered how he could ditch Ian without offending him.

They stopped by the pirate ship to watch the arm wrestling. One boy was clearly stronger but his opponent had his arm at a curious angle and was using the resulting leverage effectively so that they were at a standstill, arms shaking with effort.

Ian glanced around and paused, his attention further afield. "Huh," he said. "Don't like that."

"What did you say?"

"Nothing." Ian shrugged. "Well—I don't know. No, it's nothing."

Ian didn't seem like the type to be hesitant. "What was it that you did not like?" Osei persisted.

Ian turned his flat eyes on him. "I thought I saw something, that's all. But I may be wrong."

"What did you see?"

Ian held his gaze for a second longer than was comfortable. "OK, brother. Look over at the Double Dutch."

You are not my brother, O thought. He hated it when white people used that word, trying to take on some of the coolness of black culture without wearing the skin and paying the dues. Still, he looked across the playground. There were two sets of girls turning ropes, and two girls jumping—one of them Blanca—while others stood around watching. He could see nothing out of the ordinary; it was a scene he'd witnessed many times on different playgrounds. Girls loved to jump rope. Osei couldn't see the appeal himself. He liked to do things where you move and get somewhere, rather than staying in one place. "What am I looking at?"

"There, it's happening again. Casper."

Casper was the only boy among the girls. Right now he was picking something from a hand held out, palm up, to him. Dee's hand. O's girlfriend had returned and he hadn't noticed. And she hadn't come straight to him. And she was feeding another boy. As Osei watched, Casper popped whatever it was in his mouth.

"What was that?"

Ian narrowed his eyes at the pair. After a moment he turned back to O. "Strawberries."

Resentment pulsed through Osei, which he did his best to tamp down. The small smile that appeared briefly on Ian's face told him he had not succeeded in hiding it.

✳

It was impressive how one word could rattle the black boy so easily. With Dee haplessly appearing at the right moment with a handful of strawberries, Ian couldn't have managed it better than if he'd planned it.

O stepped toward the jump rope area, but Ian put his hand out to stop him—though he was careful not to touch that dark skin. "Let's see what they do. That's the second strawberry she's given him," he added. As they watched, Casper pulled the leaves off, popped the fruit in his mouth and grinned at Dee, who grinned back, clearly pleased.

"That must be a good strawberry," Ian remarked. "I wonder if she'll give him all of them."

O's brow crumpled briefly before he smoothed it out like a sheet on a bed. "I love strawberries," he said in a light tone that didn't fool Ian. Now he just had to push it a little further, like pressing on a bruise that doesn't seem to hurt at first.

"Those strawberries are probably from Dee's mother's garden," he said. "She grows her own, you know. They're a lot sweeter than what you get at the grocery store."

"Have you tried them?"

"Me? No. I've just heard about them." Ian decided not to explain that Dee brought some in for her class every year.

They stood in silence, watching Dee and Casper chat to each other as the girls jumped rope next to them.

"It's just like Casper to get the first taste."

Again O was quick to respond. "What do you mean?"

"Well ... he gets everything he wants, doesn't he? The girls are crazy about him—all of them."

"But—he is a nice boy. He was nice to me."

"Sure he was nice to you. That's the easiest way to get what he wants."

"What does he want?"

Ian took his time, surveying the playground and all of the activity he knew so well and would have to leave soon, to move on to older and harder playgrounds. "I don't want to say anything, since it's none of my business."

O turned to face Ian, pulling his eyes away from Dee and Casper. "What business?"

Ian shrugged, enjoying the moment. There was no need to rush this.

"If you have something to say to me, please say it now." O's dark eyes had turned fierce, though the rest of his face remained still. Ian wondered what it would be like to fight him.

"Look, it's great you're going with Dee," he said at last. "Impressive, since you're a bl—a new boy. You move fast. All in one morning! Maybe that'll work out."

"But ... I know that there is a 'but' coming."

Ian waggled his head in a gesture that wasn't a yes and wasn't a no. "Dee is probably the girl most boys want to go with in the sixth grade."

"Not Blanca?"

Ian snorted. "Too obvious. Too . . . trashy. I'm amazed Casper puts up with her."

"What about Mimi?"

Ian froze. "What about her?" He tried to sound casual.

"She is . . . interesting. She told me she has visions sometimes."

"What?"

O jerked his head at the barking sound, and Ian tried to rein himself in.

"Is she your girlfriend? I am sorry, I did not know."

Ian wondered why O felt he needed to apologize. "What did she say?"

"Nothing. It was nothing."

"What did Mimi say?" Ian repeated himself lightly, but the underlying menace was clear.

It was O's turn to shrug. "It was not a big thing. She just said that sometimes she gets headaches and a shimmering light in her vision. An aura, she called it. She said it gives her a sense that something is about to happen."

"Really." What was Mimi doing telling this black boy things she hadn't told him? They had only spoken for a minute at recess—she'd obviously packed a lot in. She must have wanted to. Ian was not interested in her headaches and her premonitions, but he didn't like others gaining access to privileged information about her.

"Anyway, you were saying about Dee . . . and Casper."

"Right." Ian forced himself to snap out of the swelling rage that threatened to overturn the trap he was carefully setting. "Casper is the most popular boy in the whole school. And Dee is—put it this way, if they were in high school they'd be voted Homecoming King and Queen. You know what that is?"

O nodded.

"They go together."

"But she is with *me*."

"Sure she is ... except she's not feeding you her strawberries, is she?"

O shook his head, like a bear puzzled by a wounded paw. "Dee is not going to change that fast over me. We have only just started going together."

"Sure, sure." Ian made as if to back off. "You're right. Forget I said anything. Besides, Dee'll probably bring in strawberries again anyway. You can have some then." He paused. "It is strange, though, that she didn't come straight to you when she got back to school. Are you sure you're going together?"

"Are you saying that she has dumped me? Already? Between the lunch bell and now?" O's voice was starting to rise.

"I'm not saying that," Ian soothed him. "I'm just saying: keep an eye on her. And watch yourself with Casper. Sure he acts nice, but that doesn't mean he *is* nice."

Ian could have said more, but there was no time— Dee had spotted O and was rushing across the playground to him. "I managed to come back early," she said when she got to him, putting a hand on his shoulder. "I told my mother there was a rehearsal for the end-of-the-year play, and she believed me!" Dee had the incredulous tone of someone who is not used to lying and is surprised that it worked. "Hey, maybe you can be in the play too."

"What are you doing?" O asked.

"Shakespeare—*A Midsummer Night's Dream.* We've been rehearsing for a while, but there are lots of parts. You could be a fairy, or one of the peasants putting on a play."

"What part are you playing?"

"Hermia—one of the lead girls."

"Doesn't she fall in love with one boy after another?" Ian interjected. "She's fickle like that. Lucky boys."

"Only because of what *you* do. It's just magic," Dee explained, as O's face darkened. "It's a comedy, so it turns out all right at the end."

"Who do *you* play?" O demanded of Ian.

"He plays Puck," Dee said. "The head fairy who makes all the mischief happen. Now, look what I've got." She held up a paper bag. "Strawberries! The first of the season. I brought some for you."

"Only for me?"

"I didn't know if you'd had them before. Do they grow strawberries in Ghana?"

"I have had them—in New York, in Europe. Not Ghana."

"Well, try one. You won't believe how sweet they are." Dee reached into her bag and held out a glistening strawberry, bright red, in a perfect heart shape.

"I am not hungry."

Dee laughed. "I eat strawberries because I like the taste. Doesn't matter if I'm hungry."

Ian was watching with satisfaction. The simple power of his words had transformed the black boy into a cold statue, the white girl hanging off him, carried along by the giddiness of her emotions so that she seemed willfully unaware of any change in her boyfriend. Ian waited to see the hurt enter her like a knife.

But then, O relaxed. "All right." He took the strawberry, grasped it by the leaves, and bit into it. After a moment he smiled. "Wow. That is *good*. Very good. Your mother grows these?"

Puzzled surprise crossed Dee's face, mingling with the pleasure she'd had at O's response. "How did you know that?"

Ian stepped forward. "Can I try one?"

"Oh. Sure." As Dee pulled a strawberry from the bag and dropped it into his outstretched hand, Ian studied O. His smooth brow furrowed again, those lines deepening as Ian bit into the strawberry and let the juice run down to his chin. It was good, Ian could tell, even though he was not fond of strawberries, or anything sweet.

"Did Casper like his strawberries too?" he asked, wiping his mouth with the back of his hand.

Dee frowned, matching her boyfriend. "Yes. Come on, let's go over to the trees." She directed this only to O, taking his hand and pulling him toward the sandpit and the cypress trees, leaving Ian alone.

Not for long, though: Rod scuttled over from where he had been waiting by the arm wrestlers on the pirate ship. "Did it work?" he asked, his longing look following the couple. "It doesn't look like it did!"

Ian considered O and Dee, holding hands under the trees as she fed him another strawberry; and Casper, watching Blanca with a proprietary air as she jumped Double Dutch. They were like characters in a play who needed an extra scene, a thread to pull them tight. And Ian held that thread. It would be satisfying to take them all down—not just the black boy, but the golden boy and golden girl of the school too. Casper and Dee were like the Teflon pan his mother used to fry eggs in—nothing stuck to them. He had never been able to touch them—they were on a level above Ian's kind of activity. Everyone admired them in a way he would never experience. It would be an end-of-school present to himself if he could conquer them. Of course, there was a clear danger that he could fall with them; but the risk of that was as exhilarating as the power he wielded.

He glanced at Rod, so eager to take part, and made a quick decision. "Go over to Casper and say something to him to make him hit you," he improvised. "But don't say anything about me telling you to if the teachers ask you afterward. Which they will."

Rod's mouth dropped open. "What? Why? I don't want to get hurt! And what does Casper have to do with it, anyway?"

"It's indirect—the best way. The black boy won't know you or I have anything to do with it."

"To do with what?"

"We need him to think Dee is two-timing him with Casper. The best way to do that is to get Dee to talk about Casper a lot to O. To defend him. It'll drive O crazy. He's already a little suspicious of Casper. This will push him over the edge."

Rod shook his head as if dazed. "I don't understand what you're talking about—it's too complicated. Why don't we just hit the black boy?"

"Because that won't accomplish anything. You don't want him being the victim—it will just make Dee like him more." Ian was having a hard time explaining a strategy he had not fully figured out himself, but felt in his gut would work. He had always been a good judge of such things. "Look, you want a chance with Dee or not?"

Rod gazed at Dee and O, who were now sitting on the sand. O had his arm at her back and was laughing, teeth bright white against his black skin. Rod turned to Ian. "What can I say to him? Casper never gets mad."

"Say something about Blanca. Something dirty."

Rod's red cheeks flushed deeper.

"I'm sure you can think of something," Ian added. "Go on. Just do it. Otherwise that new boy will have stolen your girl. Is that what you want? A *black boy* going with Dee? Trust me—that will keep happening unless you fight Casper."

Rod took a deep breath, pumped his fists, and stumbled toward the girls jumping rope.

Ian sighed. It would have been better to have someone more reliable doing his work for him.

He knew he shouldn't be openly watching Rod and Casper now—that could give away who was behind the fight. Plus it would be painful seeing Rod make a mess of it—which he was likely to do. If he did, Ian would deny any involvement, and with his word against Rod's, he knew he would always win.

He walked over to the arm wrestling on the ship. The boys had made it into a kind of tournament, with two sets simultaneously competing in the semifinal round. Ian watched as two boys won and turned to face each other.

"Taking bets now," Ian announced. When he set up betting he took a 40 percent cut of the candy or money handed over, arguing that he was taking the risk of being suspended if any of the teachers caught them. He was surprised sometimes that no one argued with his high cut. They seemed afraid to haggle with him.

The wrestlers and spectators whipped their heads around at Ian's voice, and a wave of unease rippled through them. Irritation as well, some boys clearly feeling their fun had just been tainted. Ian noted those looks, for future reference.

"C'mon, don't you want to make this more fun?" he continued. "Otherwise it's boring—just an arm wrestle. You'll care more about who wins if you bet."

He didn't get to see how much he would have made from the betting, as shouts from across the playground interrupted them. "Fight! Fight!"

The boys abandoned the pirate ship en masse and ran like rats to join a ring that had formed in the jump rope area. Fights occurred every few weeks, and were the highlight of playground entertainment, especially if you weren't in it yourself. Ian followed more slowly, for he knew who the opponents were, and what he would see.

✳

Dee had just finished taking her hair out of its braids for Osei when they heard the familiar chant: "Fight! Fight!" They looked at each other, but the call was too strong. Reluctantly getting to their feet, they went to join the spectators.

Dee was astonished to find it was Casper and Rod facing each other inside the ring of students. Casper was never in fights.

"What did you say?" he was yelling.

"You heard me," Rod replied, bouncing nervously on the balls of his feet.

"Take it back," Casper demanded.

"No. It's true!"

"Casper, don't let him say that!" Blanca cried. She was standing near him, with Mimi holding on to her to keep her from barging in between the boys.

"Take. It. Back."

"No!" Rod seemed to lunge toward him, feinting a blow, and Casper returned with a punch, as much to block him as to hit him. His fist landed true, right in Rod's face, and he went down immediately. The crowd gasped, and Blanca began to scream. Rod lay on his back, clutching his eye as the victor stood over him, fists still clenched, looking confused, as if he couldn't take in what he'd just done.

Dee glanced at Osei beside her. He was watching Casper with a look she could not quite read: surprise, fascination, and something else. Wariness. Distance. Judgment. A darkness she had glimpsed momentarily when Osei first refused to eat one of her strawberries.

Blanca was busy screaming while being propped up by Mimi. Dee knew she should go to her, but held back, not wanting to get dragged into the drama. Blanca would be talking about it till the end of the school year, and maybe into junior high.

Two teachers were quickly on the scene—Miss Lode helping Rod to his feet, pressing damp brown paper towels to his eye and leading him away to see the school nurse; Mr. Brabant grasping the culprit by the arms and frogmarching him toward the entrance, Casper with his head bowed.

Once they were gone, the ring of spectators remained in groups, discussing what had happened. Dee listened in on the conversations around her.

"Rod didn't do anything—Casper just hit him!"

"He must have done *something*."

"Can you believe *Casper* doing that? He's never in fights! I don't think he's been in a fight all the years he's been here."

"Why would he risk his reputation doing something so stupid?"

"Rod said something to him. I saw. He went up to him and said something."

"What'd he say?"

"Must have been pretty bad for him to have that reaction."

"Really bad."

"The worst."

"I heard Rod said something about Blanca."

"No, it was about his mother."

"What about his mother?"

"Who knows?"

Mimi gave her a desperate look, and Dee left O to join her in helping with the hysterical Blanca. As Casper was being taken away by Mr. Brabant, Blanca wailed even louder. Anyone would think *she* had been hit rather than Rod.

Dee lost her patience. "For God's sake, Blanca, can't you be quieter about it?" Even as she said it, she heard in the back of her mind her mother telling her not to take the Lord's name in vain.

Blanca sniffed. "Easy for you to say, Little Miss Perfect. It wasn't *you* who had awful things said about you. It wasn't *your* boyfriend who had to defend you. It wasn't *your* boyfriend who will probably be suspended!"

Mimi gestured with her head, and they led Blanca to a quieter corner, their charge allowing them to now that Casper and Rod were gone and her audience was dispersing.

"What exactly did Rod say?" Dee demanded.

"I can't repeat it—it's too awful!"

"Blanca, we can't help you if you don't tell us," Dee persisted.

Blanca leaned against the brick wall of the school. "He said—he said ..." She stopped, her mouth trembling, and caught back a sob. This time she seemed genuinely upset.

"Take a deep breath, then blow it out," Mimi ordered. Dee admired her firmness in the face of so much emotion. And it worked: Blanca took a shaky breath, breathed out, and calmed down.

"Just repeat what he said fast—all in one go."

"Rod said I was trashy and had let Casper go all the way with me. But I didn't!" Blanca covered her face with her hands, clearly embarrassed to have repeated such an accusation.

Dee almost snorted, but held it back. Boys said things like that about girls all the time. Why was this time any different?

As if reading her thoughts, Blanca dropped her hands and added, "He said it so loud, in front of all the girls. In front of fourth graders! It's *so* embarrassing! And now that Casper's hit him, *everyone's* talking about it. And they're all going to think I'm trashy!"

"Blanca, it's *Casper* you should be worried about," Dee retorted. "*He's* the one who may be suspended." She could not imagine what it must be like to be suspended; her own school record was unblemished, as Casper's had been until now. Blanca, she recalled, was suspended in fifth grade for wearing hip-huggers to school that showed off not only her belly button but her hip bones too. Only students like Rod had been suspended regularly, for throwing rocks or setting fire to leaves on the playground.

Blanca was looking at her strangely. "What happened to your braids?" She must have been recovering to ask such a thing.

"Osei wanted to see my hair loose," Dee replied, embarrassed. The braids had made her hair wavy, and it sprang out from her head like a hippie's. Her mother would be angry if she saw it. Dee would have to rebraid it before she went home.

"By the way, Dee, you dropped your—" Mimi broke off as Ian approached.

"You all right, Blanca?" he said.

Blanca wiped her eyes with the back of her hand. "I am upset," she replied, mustering a dignity that made Dee want to smile because it was so out of keeping with her usual ebullience. "And I'm worried about Casper," she added. "He might be suspended!"

"Rod's an idiot," Ian said. "It's just a shame what Casper did. No one will trust him now—not even his friends. Like your boyfriend." He nodded at Dee.

"What do you mean?"

"He was really shocked. Casper had been so nice to him—you know, he didn't have to be nice to a bl—a new boy. So O doesn't know what to think now he's seen Casper's other side."

"Casper doesn't have an 'other side'!" Dee protested.

"Tell that to your boyfriend, then, 'cause he's confused."

"I will."

Mimi was frowning at Ian. Dee had been surprised when she'd found out they were going together. They were so different: Mimi was unusual, sensitive; Ian—well, he was a bully, though he had never bothered Dee except for once in third grade when he had smeared paste on her skirt and told her he was going to chase her home, and even then it had felt almost like he was going through a list and being mean to everyone, one by one.

Now it bothered her that Ian seemed to have inside information about Osei. While Dee approved of her boyfriend becoming friends with Casper, seeing him talking to Ian had made her uneasy. Dee didn't dislike Ian, exactly, but she didn't trust him either.

This made her more determined to talk to O about Casper. He would be much better off hanging out with Casper than with Ian. She would reassure him that Casper's hitting Rod was out of character, that he had done it to defend Blanca. O would understand that, she was sure. He too was honorable.

She left Mimi and Blanca and Ian to get in line. A few other classmates were standing behind Osei, but without a word they stepped back to let her in. She smiled at O, and was startled when he didn't return it, his expression stern. *He must be wondering about Casper*, she thought. *At least this I can fix.*

"Don't worry," she reassured him. "I bet they won't suspend Casper. Once they hear what Rod said about Blanca . . ." she trailed off, stunned by the ugly look that flashed across O's face.

"Why would I be worried about Casper?"

"Well, he's a friend."

"Of yours, maybe. Not of mine."

"Of course he's your friend!"

O grimaced. "Dee, I have been here for one morning. *No one* is my friend." He softened when he saw her face fall. "Well, you, of course. But I do not know anyone else enough to be friends with them. I am the new boy—the new *black* boy. I will be lucky to get through the day without getting beaten up."

"You're exaggerating. The teachers wouldn't let that happen."

Osei sighed. "Dee, I am going to tell you a story about teachers. When I was at school in New York, a teacher asked me to give a report on Ghana to the class. Not just a short report like what I did for your class this morning, but longer. I was to report on its history, its culture, what crops it produces and exports. All of the facts, you see. So I gathered information. Some of it I knew anyway, and I also went to the library and read about it, and I asked my parents too. And then I gave the report. And do you know what grade the teacher gave me for all that work? A D! If she could have given me an F I think she would have, but you get an F when you do not do the work at all, and I had clearly done the work."

"Why did she give you a D?"

"She thought I was making up some of it."

"What were you making up?"

"I did not make up any of it! Part of my report was about slavery. You know many Ghanaians were captured by slave traders and taken to America and the West Indies."

"I—yes," Dee answered, because it was easier to. She had not known slaves came from Ghana, though they had probably been taught it and she had forgotten. "So . . . that's not made up, what you said."

"No. But I also explained that there were chiefs of tribes who made deals with the white traders and handed over some of their people in order for the rest of the tribe to be left alone. And the teacher thought I was lying, and gave me a D. She even called me a racist against my own people."

"So that's true? The chiefs did that?" Dee tried to hide her surprise.

"Yes, yes, but that is not the point."

"What did you do? Did you get your parents to speak to her?"

Osei did not answer for a moment, a grim smile crossing his face. "It was my *father* who suggested I tell the class about the tribal chiefs, to make the story more balanced, so that they would not feel so bad about the slavery part. To be *diplomatic*. I said nothing to my parents. I was not going to tell him what happened to his diplomacy. So you see, even the teachers are not on my side, but are looking for ways to trip me. I cannot trust teachers, or students."

"That's not true! You can trust me. You can trust Mimi—she's my best friend." Dee pushed from her mind the warning Mimi had given her about going with O. "And you can trust Casper," she added.

"Why do you say him? He just gave someone a black eye for no reason."

"He did have a good reason for hitting Rod—he was defending Blanca. I bet you would too, if someone said the things about me that were said about her."

At last—something that worked. O stood a little straighter, the better to step into his role as noble, protecting boyfriend. "I would give them *two* black eyes."

Dee slid her hand into his and laced their fingers together as they moved forward with the line to head up to their classroom. "Then you'll understand why we have to support Casper. He didn't do anything wrong."

O seemed to slump, and made to pull his hand away, but Dee held on to it—until Mr. Brabant frowned at her and shook his head. If she weren't careful she too might be suspended. She let go of O's hand.

As she followed him up the stairs to their classroom, her teacher stopped her. Dee wanted to call out to Osei to stop too, but Mr. Brabant might tell them both off for holding hands. She knew he didn't like the new boy and would use any opportunity to show it.

But Mr. Brabant surprised her. "What has happened to your hair?" he demanded.

"Oh! I—I took out the braids." Dee blushed. Mr. Brabant had never said anything about her hair; but then, he had not had reason to. Until now, she had kept it bound up and tidy.

"It looks messy."

Dee opened her mouth to apologize, then stopped, recalling her earlier defiance on the playground with Mr. Brabant. "It's not against the dress code to wear my hair like this."

Mr. Brabant frowned. "No, but it's not like you."

Dee shrugged. "I like it this way."

"Do you?"

"Yes." Actually it tickled her neck and kept getting in her mouth, but Dee was not going to tell him that.

"That's a shame, because it doesn't suit you. Trust me."

Dee hung her head, not wanting to meet her teacher's eye. She felt as if she were being told off by her father.

"All right. Go on up to the classroom."

Dee hurried away, holding back a shudder.

At their desks, she could not help glancing at Casper's empty seat at the cluster of desks next to hers, hoping he would magically reappear. She could hear Blanca, sniffing back tears across the room, taking advantage of a new setting in which to play out her drama.

"That's enough, Blanca," Mr. Brabant said. "Settle down. Let's leave playground events out of the classroom. Now, pop quiz on the American presidents. Get out your pencils. Osei, you can take it too, though I won't record your grade. It will show you where your gaps of knowledge are so that you can start filling them. You may only be in my class for a month, but it won't be wasted time."

Dee frowned. She wanted to chide him for assuming O wouldn't know about American presidents just because he was African. She wished she could stand up for her boyfriend the way Casper had stood up for Blanca. But she couldn't, not after how Mr. Brabant had just spoken to her. Besides, Osei didn't seem bothered by the assumption: he simply nodded and brought her Snoopy pencil case out from his desk, surprising her for a moment until she remembered their swap.

She reached into her bag and came up with—nothing. She rummaged around, pushing aside books, a cardigan, a pack of tissues, a little bag of jacks. No strawberry case. She opened her desk lid, knowing it wasn't there but looking anyway. She could feel O's eyes on her.

"Can I borrow a pencil?" she whispered.

"Don't you have the strawberry case?"

"I do." Dee answered too quickly, she knew, and tried to pace her next words. "I took it home at lunch and must have left it there. In fact, I remember now—I showed it to my mother. It'll be on the kitchen table."

She would never have shown the case to her mother, who would have said it was too frivolous and taken it away. Dee had had to keep the Snoopy case hidden for that reason.

As she took the pencil Osei offered, she found she couldn't look him in the eye. Already she'd told him her first lie.

PART IV

AFTERNOON RECESS

Teddy bear, teddy bear
Turn around
Teddy bear, teddy bear
Touch the ground
Teddy bear, teddy bear
Show your shoe
Teddy bear, teddy bear
That will do

Teddy bear, teddy bear
Go upstairs
Teddy bear, teddy bear
Say your prayers
Teddy bear, teddy bear
Turn out the light
Teddy bear, teddy bear
Say good night!

Mimi pulled Ian aside as they were heading out to afternoon recess. He was not expecting her to do such a thing. She was not the type to initiate—and in front of their classmates. Separating him from the rest like that made him look weak and out of control. It was the sort of thing he should do to her, to show everyone who was in charge. Annoyed, he stood apart from her in the hall. "What?" If he didn't get out to the playground quickly, the kickball teams would form without him being captain.

"I wanted to say something." Mimi had that soft look girls got when they wanted to talk about their feelings. Ian shuddered. That was the last thing he needed right now.

He cut her off. "Did you get something of Dee's?"

Mimi paused and ran her tongue over her braces, clearly thrown off the track she had been about to head down. She was looking pinched and unhappy, and her face was blotchy. "I did." She continued to hesitate.

"Well? What did you get?"

Mimi pulled from her bag a pink plastic rectangle with strawberries dotted on it.

"What the hell is that?" Ian demanded. "It's ugly, whatever it is." His tone made her cringe, which was what he wanted—it put him back in the driver's seat.

"It's Osei's—the new boy's pencil case. He gave it to Dee. She accidentally dropped it and I picked it up. I know you said you wanted something Casper gave to Dee, but will this do instead?"

Ian's attention swung onto the pencil case like a spotlight moving to rest on a character onstage. Mimi shifted uneasily. He smiled. This was exactly the right thing, and she had no idea that it was. Mimi did not think strategically like him. She had no understanding of the playground and how it worked, and how disturbing the appearance of a boy like O could be to its natural order. It wouldn't occur to her to try to fix things the way Ian was going to. Really she should be thanking him.

"Who knows you have it?"

"No one."

"Good." Ian held out his hand. "Give it to me."

There was a long pause as Mimi stood, holding the pencil case and looking like a trapped animal—an animal that has willingly walked into the trap and now regrets it. Ian waited patiently; in the end she would give it to him.

But first came the bargaining, which he had not expected, nor what she asked for. "I don't want to go with you anymore," she said. "I'll only give it to you if you agree to break up with me, and leave me alone."

Her face was full of misery—a long way from the pink cheeks and flare of interest by the flagpole a few days before.

Ian hid his irritation. Nor would he ever let her think he was hurt at being rejected, or wanted to know what she didn't like about him. For he already knew what it was: they were nothing alike. He was hard and she was strange.

It was not that he liked her much. But Ian did not want the others to find out Mimi had dumped him. Later he would spread the word among the boys that she had refused to go all the way with him. Or maybe he would say she'd done it with him, and then he'd dumped her. He would have to think about how to get the best out of this situation. Still, he wanted the pencil case. "All right," he said.

Mimi didn't move. "You don't badmouth me, or say things like what Rod said about Blanca." It was as if she'd heard his thoughts.

"I won't say anything. And you won't say anything either," he added, then gestured impatiently. "Now, are you gonna give it to me or not?"

Mimi bit her lip. As she held out the case, he could see that her hand was shaking. She was not good at this sort of negotiation, had held nothing back to keep him in line. He would have no problem turning the breakup in his favor.

"Go on out," he said, taking the case. "I'll be there in a little while."

Mimi was staring at the pencil case, now safe in Ian's hands. She looked frightened, her eyes sparking with the strange flecks that made them swirl. "What are you going to do with it?"

But Ian was already turning into the cloakroom attached to their class. "Nothing for you to worry about," he said over his shoulder. As he rummaged on the coat hooks for his jacket, he could feel her still in the hall, and gritted his teeth. "Idiot," he muttered. He now felt miles removed from the desire he'd had for her at the flagpole. He found his jacket—plain, navy blue, unused for the past few weeks as it had grown warmer. Before pocketing his new possession, he unzipped the case to look inside. There wasn't much of interest: pencils of various lengths and colors, a couple erasers, a plastic pencil sharpener, a short ruler, a dime, a piece of Bazooka bubble gum, a scrap of paper, a plastic egg full of Silly Putty. He kept the dime, unwrapped the gum—dropping the brightly colored comic that came with it without reading it—and stuffed it in his mouth. He glanced at the paper: written in a peculiar loopy style was O's name, address, and phone number. He envisaged the crank phone calls he could make and smiled; the opportunities had been handed to him on a platter.

Ian dumped everything else into a cardboard box full of a jumble of classroom detritus: broken chalk, old blackboard erasers, gray metal bookends, scraps of construction paper. He pulled a sheaf of leftover mimeographed worksheets on the main agricultural products of the United States (corn, wheat, cotton, beef) over the case's contents. No one would find them for weeks, until Miss Lode cleaned out the cloakroom when school finished for the summer. He would be long gone by then—on to another school and other victims.

Once it was empty, Ian examined the case. God, it was hideous. Only a girl could stand to use something as lurid as this. The only interesting features were the embossed strawberries, with knobbly points poking up from the plastic that reminded him of nipples. He had seen nipples dimpled like that in the copies of *Playboy* he'd stolen over the years. The girls' nipples he'd caught glimpses of—when he spied on them changing for gym, or the fifth grader he'd pressured into lifting her top for him—were tiny and smooth like birds' beaks. Ian touched one of the knobbly strawberries and smiled as the sensation traveled to his groin. Maybe this was why the black boy had had the pencil case, if it had the same effect on him.

He mustn't keep it, however. It would be much more useful in stirring things up out on the playground rather than exciting him in the cloakroom. Ian could get that feeling from other things. What could he do with the case, though? It needed to be in Casper's possession to have the most effect on O, as concrete evidence that would confirm the suspicions Ian had already planted. But Casper wouldn't carry around something like that; no boy with any self-respect would hold on to a pink plastic pencil case covered with strawberries.

If not Casper, then someone close to him. *Yes.* Ian smiled and nodded to himself, knowing now what to do. Shrugging on his jacket—it would be warm outside but he needed a hiding place—he tucked the case in the inside pocket and headed outside.

The sixth graders had gathered for their afternoon game, when girls and boys played together. The usual captains—Casper and Ian—not being there, two alternatives had taken on the roles: Rod—and O, to Ian's surprise. How could a new, black boy have wormed his way into the playground hierarchy so quickly and easily? Ian expected more of his classmates, but they seemed to be pussies, willingly rolling over and allowing the new boy to dominate. Ian would have to act fast, or O would take over completely.

The moment Rod spotted Ian, he ran over, calling, "Ian! Ian's on my team." The skin around his right eye was turning inky blue where Casper had punched him, but he was otherwise intact. Ian felt a moment's disgust.

"I got detention," Rod whispered when he was close. "Mrs. Duke said she would've suspended me except the black eye is punishment enough. It hurts!"

"Did you mention me?"

"No, I said I wouldn't and I didn't."

"Good."

"Hey, it's not your turn, Rod!" a couple others cried. "It's O's turn."

Ian stood waiting as O considered which student to pick next for his team. He had already chosen a few others, including Dee and Mimi. Despite his antipathy to the black boy, when O's eyes came to rest on Ian, the attention thrilled him—positive attention, unlike the cringing unease he was more accustomed to from the others.

O nodded at him. "Ian."

Ian nodded back, and walked over to join the team as Rod muttered, "Damn!"

While O and Rod continued picking teammates, Ian found what he was looking for: Blanca, sitting alone on the pirate ship, sulking. She would not be playing but preferred to lick her wounds very publicly. Perfect.

They lost the toss and went out to field. Ian didn't wait for O to tell him what position to take, but headed to the outfield, close to the pirate ship near third base. Luckily Dee was far from him on the other side of the outfield, and O had his back to Ian, pitching. They were unlikely to spot the strawberry case. Ian was able to sidle over to Blanca, who sat with her arms across one of the bars on the ship deck, her head leaning on one arm. She had her platform sandals up on the lower bar, and if Ian were at a different angle he could see up her skirt. He didn't move to a better spot, however, for he needed to concentrate. "Blanca," he whispered.

When she didn't respond, he said her name a little louder. She glanced over, indifferent. Throughout their years at school together, Ian had never been able to control or scare her. Blanca was too self-absorbed to be afraid of him; she had her own force and created her own calamities. Ian was nothing to her—or had been nothing. Now he would change that.

"I've got something for you," he continued, then paused, taking his time. A girl kicked the ball straight to the shortstop for the first out, and Ian clapped along with his teammates. "From Casper," he added eventually.

Blanca snapped her head up and let her feet drop to the ship deck. "What?" she cried.

"Shhh. It's a secret—something just for you." Ian didn't want her drawing attention to herself just yet—not until he was safely out of the picture. He moved closer. "I saw him when he went to the bathroom while he was in the principal's office. He asked me to give this to you." Ian pulled out the pencil case from his jacket pocket and handed it to her.

Blanca breathed out. "Ohhh. It's so cute!" She ran her fingers over the strawberries just the way Ian had. "Wait till I show the other girls!"

"Don't! Not yet."

"Why not?"

A boy kicked the ball toward the outfield in between first and second and ran to first base.

"Casper wanted it to be a secret between you two— something only you and he share. Just for now. Besides, you should thank him first before you show it to everyone else." With any luck Casper wouldn't be back for a few days, and by then the damage to O and Dee would have been done, if Ian could show the black boy who had his case. He was freewheeling, he knew, like cycling down a hill without touching the brakes. But that was part of the fun, knowing he could crash.

"OK . . ." Blanca looked puzzled. "Is Casper all right? Has he been suspended?"

"I don't know," Ian was able to answer honestly.

"Is he worried about me? He should be. I have to be out here with everybody knowing what Rod said about me." When Ian didn't make the sympathetic noises she was expecting, she added, "It's awful! It's so hard being a girl. You have no idea." She tossed her dark curls for emphasis.

"I'm sure it is," Ian agreed, because it was easier to.

Rod was up. "Make sure you get that jerk out," Blanca hissed. "I could kill him for hurting Casper!"

As if her words were a magnet, Rod kicked the ball high toward Ian. Another time he might have deliberately fumbled the ball, but now he stepped forward to meet it, catching it with a satisfying thump against his chest. Blanca cheered as loudly as if she had been on their team, which filled Ian with unexpected pride.

They got a third out easily and switched sides, heading in to kick with Rod's team going out to field. As O's team gathered around their captain to hear the order of the kickers, Ian murmured to him, "Usually we let a girl kick first. You could ask Dee. Everyone will expect you to choose her to go first."

O nodded. "Dee, then Duncan, then Ian, me, and . . ." He pointed to the rest of the teammates in order.

Up first to kick, Dee made her usual short bunt and dash to first base, where Rod was baseman. She stood as far from him as she could, to demonstrate her disdain at his part in insulting Blanca and inflaming Casper. In fact, most of the girls were freezing him out, even the ones he had chosen for his team. Rod hung his head, clearly unhappy with his new role as playground pariah. Ian was smirking about it as he went to stand next to O.

But now he must get to work. "You've put together a good team."

"Thanks." O had his eyes on Duncan, the next kicker.

"I see Blanca's got something from Casper," Ian remarked. "I guess he's pretty crazy about her, giving her a present."

"Huh." O was not paying attention. Ian would have to be more obvious.

"I never thought of her as a *strawberry* girl, somehow," he said. "She prefers cherry Now and Laters, if the color of her lips is anything to go by."

O turned to him. "What kind of girl?"

"Strawberry."

"What about strawberries?" There was an edge to O's voice that made Ian want to smile with satisfaction that his quarry had taken the bait so easily. However, he was careful to keep his face neutral.

"She has a new pencil case, with strawberries on it. Said Casper gave it to her. Wants to play with it rather than join the game." He shrugged. "Girls."

"Where?"

Ian pointed. Blanca was still sitting on the pirate ship, and had the case in her lap, zipping and unzipping it. If you weren't looking for it, you wouldn't notice it—as indeed, Dee didn't, over on first base. Nor did Mimi, waiting on the bench with the other kickers. But O already knew what he was looking for. And when he saw that flash of pink in Blanca's lap, he went very still—so still he didn't watch Duncan kick the ball far past second base and get to first, with Dee on second.

Ian began to think he was not going to have to do much more—the poison was taking hold, and he could simply stand back and watch it spread. He just had to be careful to seem detached, and deny any involvement.

His work done, he was able to step up to the plate for his turn with a lightness he had not felt all day—all week, all year. He gazed out at the field full of a team of players that by rights should have been his rather than Rod's and thought: *I am going to kick a home run now, to show you all just how much I rule this place.* He aimed for the farthest corner of the playground, ran to meet the ball rolled at him, and sent it to his target.

※

Whenever someone managed to kick a home run, any players on the bases made a ritual of walking, dancing, or skipping around them, laughing and shouting on their way to home plate glory and rubbing it in to the other team. Dee skipped, thrilled that Osei's team was already scoring three runs and was likely to win decisively. His first game as captain and this was the result. An excellent start. *He's gonna be fine at this school,* she thought. *And he's my boyfriend.*

She skipped up to home plate, jumping on it with both feet, then began slapping fives with her teammates. When Duncan ran up to home plate behind her, he held out a hand. "Gimme five," he said.

Dee slapped his hand, palm to palm.

"On the black hand side." They slapped the backs of their hands together.

"In the hole." Each made a fist and bumped the tops and bottoms.

"You got soul!" They shook hands with thumbs clasped, as they had seen black people do on TV.

Dee was grinning until she caught sight of Osei, who

had watched their ritual with his face set to expressionless. Dee blushed. "Oh, Osei, I—" She stopped, embarrassed, not just because, viewed through his eyes, the gimme five ritual now seemed a ludicrous display between two white kids trying to act cool, but because he had turned away from her and walked up to home plate. There he stood, rigid, waiting for the ball to be returned to the pitcher.

Dee stared, startled out of the joy she had just felt at scoring. Surely he couldn't be mad at her because of some stupid hand-slapping? Was it offensive to say "black hand side" if you were white? Watching his angry back, she was so confused she wanted to cry.

"He's upset about Casper, that's all," she heard behind her. Ian had made the rounds of the bases and was standing nearby, his usually muddy gray eyes bright, his cheeks red. He held out his hand, palm up.

She gave him five, to be polite. Ian curved his fingers slightly and pulled them across her palm. It felt so creepy that Dee jerked her hand back, then worried he might be offended. "That was a great kick," she said, then wondered why she felt the need to placate him.

"Thanks. I'm sure you can make him feel better about Casper."

"I . . ." *Is that really what the problem is?* Dee thought but did not say, as she did not want to talk to Ian about Osei.

"It's hard having a black boyfriend," Ian went on, relentless. "Most girls wouldn't do that. You need all the help you can get. If Casper and Osei became friends, it would be easier for you. With someone like Casper on your side, you could do whatever you wanted—go with a chimpanzee if you wanted."

Dee opened her mouth, then stopped. He was giving her a small smile. "I like your hair like that," he added.

Dee turned from him in confusion. Was he saying Osei was a chimpanzee? No, he wasn't, she decided as she went to sit on the team bench, but the remark felt wrong, like milk that has gone slightly off but doesn't smell yet. She wasn't sure how to counter it, though, as Ian seemed honestly to want to help.

Osei's kick was desultory after Ian's home run. He made it to first base, though, and stood there, not looking in her direction, but across the field toward the pirate ship where Blanca sat. Dee frowned. Something wasn't right and she didn't know what. She wished Ian would stop staring at her.

"Casper!" Blanca shrieked. Jumping off the pirate ship, she pelted over to the chain-link fence, across from Casper's house. He had come out onto the front porch. Murmurs arose among the kids playing kickball.

"I've never seen Blanca run so fast. I'm not sure I've ever seen her run at all!"

"So he *has* been suspended!"

"How long for, do you think?"

"I can't believe Casper's gone home and it's not even the end of the day!"

"He's gonna miss the grammar test."

"Is there a test?"

"You idiot, Brabant's been warning us about it all week!"

"I wish I'd gone home instead of Casper."

"Wow, with one punch he's ruined his perfect record."

"His mom must be so mad."

"Bet his father will spank him when he gets home."

"I wonder if he'll use a belt like Ian's father does."

"Ian's father uses a belt?"

"That's what I heard."

"Oh God, look what they're doing!"

"What's she holding?"

"His dick?"

"Very funny. Oh—she dropped it."

As they talked, the students watched Blanca and Casper. She had beckoned him to come off his porch and across the street to her. They were now kissing through the chain-link fence.

"Good thing there's a fence between them or they'd be all over each other," Jennifer muttered to Dee on the bench. "Casper must be in shock or he'd never let Blanca kiss him in front of everyone like that. She's such a show-off."

Dee smirked as she knew Jennifer expected her to, but couldn't bring herself to watch. It would hurt to see two kids acting so genuinely passionate, when she and Osei seemed already to have moved past that, way too fast.

She wanted to go and sit with Mimi, who was alone at the end of the bench, leaning back with her eyes shut. Her friend was being strange with her: not mean or angry, but distant. When Dee had asked what was wrong she said she had the tail end of a headache. That didn't feel like the whole truth.

Dee looked around. Apart from Mimi, the sixth

graders—Osei, Jennifer, Rod, Duncan, Patty—were still staring at Blanca and Casper. Only Ian was not; he was looking at Osei, and smiling.

Why does everything feel off? she thought. *This morning was so happy, but now . . .*

At least the fourth grade girls jumping rope were oblivious. Dee could hear them behind her, while reciting one of her least favorite chants:

> Teddy bear, teddy bear
> Turn around
> Teddy bear, teddy bear
> Touch the ground
> Teddy bear, teddy bear
> Show your shoe
> Teddy bear, teddy bear
> That will do
>
> Teddy bear, teddy bear
> Go upstairs
> Teddy bear, teddy bear
> Say your prayers
> Teddy bear, teddy bear
> Turn out the light
> Teddy bear, teddy bear
> Say good night!

The words were so relentless and repetitive that Dee had to resist the urge to go over and slap the girls quiet. She shook her head, surprised at herself. Whatever poison was spreading across the playground, it had infected her too.

✳

Osei would never have called himself an angry person. He had come across plenty of angry students in the schools he had gone to: angry at teachers for being unfair, at parents for saying no, at friends for being disloyal. Some even expressed anger at world events such as the Vietnam War or Nixon and his Watergate cronies. And his sister, Sisi, of course, was often angry now. Over the past year she had complained about honkies, about politicians, about black Americans putting down Africans and Africans being too reliant on Western aid. She even complained that Martin Luther King Jr. had been too passive. Sometimes their father debated with her; and he ordered her never to say such a disrespectful thing again about Martin Luther King. Her anger was so wearing, though, that often her parents simply exchanged glances, and once O was surprised to see his mother roll her eyes—a gesture he'd thought was reserved for girls. "Righteous," his mother called Sisi's tempers, and did not mean it as a compliment.

But O himself was slow to anger, he thought. As his father liked to remind him, anger was the easy option. It was much harder to keep your temper and sort out a problem with measured words and deeds. That was what a diplomat was trained to do, what his father assumed Osei would do too when he grew up—that or become an engineer. Not surprisingly, he never suggested Sisi should train to be a diplomat.

So O was surprised with himself when the anger began to well up in him like water rising steadily in a river. For a while it was hard to see, then suddenly the water was in places it wasn't meant to be—fields, roads, houses, schools, playgrounds. It was there and you couldn't get rid of it or make it change direction.

It had begun with Dee feeding Casper strawberries, had risen as she defended Casper to him. But the tipping point, when the water suddenly broke the banks and overflowed, was seeing the strawberry pencil case in Blanca's hands. Partly it was the incongruity—that a white stranger could be holding something O so strongly associated with his sister, back when she was younger, happier, more communicative, more sisterly. Now it was being passed around the playground, untethered from its personal history, as if it didn't matter that it had belonged to Sisi—as if Sisi didn't matter, when actually she mattered to Osei more than anyone. More than Dee, he realized. Dee had not yet earned her place in his heart. Now he was not sure she ever would.

For she had lied to him. Dee had told him the case was at home when clearly it was not. She had given it away, or thrown it away, and somehow it had ended up with Blanca. Casper's girlfriend. Of course, Casper was connected somewhere. Osei didn't know how but he sensed it, and Ian had confirmed it. And Dee's lying and Casper's involvement were pushing at him, building up a pressure in his head that was sure to blow.

On first base, he had watched Blanca sitting on the pirate ship with the strawberry case in her lap; she was running her fingers over the strawberries just like every other girl did. Then she'd raced over to Casper and he'd had to witness their public display, rammed up against the fence, the pencil case in her hand as they kissed until she dropped it. That brought his rage right to the surface. It only needed someone to set it free.

That someone was Dee. When the bell rang for the end of recess, Blanca and Casper kept kissing, the pencil case remained abandoned on the ground, and Dee came running over to him.

"Osei, what—" But she did not get a chance to finish. He did not want to have to confront her, to have her get in his face, talking to him, telling more lies, treating him like her boyfriend and then like the black boy on the white playground. The black sheep, with a black mark against his name. Blackballed. Blackmailed. Blacklisted. Blackhearted. It was a black day.

The dam holding back his anger broke. "Leave me alone!" he shouted, and shoved her hard—so hard that Dee flailed her arms, circling them like a cartoon character grabbing at the air, before falling backward. The sickening sound of her head cracking against the asphalt made people at last turn from the compelling Blanca-and-Casper show to a new drama.

"Dee!" Mimi cried, racing over to kneel by her friend. Dee was lying flat, eyes closed. "Dee, are you all right?" When Mimi brushed her hair from her face, her eyelids fluttered, and she opened her eyes.

O hovered over them, suddenly ashamed, sickened and helpless.

Dee looked around, confused, until her eyes met Osei's, and she flinched. "I'm OK."

Mimi looked up. "What is the *matter* with you?" she hissed at Osei. "Are you crazy? Why'd you do that?"

Osei shuddered, full of self-disgust. But his anger had not subsided; it stopped his mouth and feet so that he simply stood, silent, hands at his sides.

Hearing footsteps behind him, he knew it would be the teachers. He shut his eyes, just for a moment, though he knew it wouldn't get him what he wanted, which was to be spirited far away from this playground and these white people, especially these white adults who would be all over him now—telling him off, sending him to the principal, suspending him and calling his parents. He thought of his mother's face when she heard what he had done and felt ill.

"What's happened here?" Miss Lode knelt on the other side of Dee. "Are you hurt, Dee?"

"O pushed Dee!" Rod cried, indignant, from the crowd of students who had gathered. "He knocked her over, the black bastard!"

"Language, Rod," Miss Lode warned.

"But he did!"

"That's enough. The color of his skin has nothing to do with this. Dee, can you sit up?" She and Mimi helped Dee into a sitting position. She still seemed dazed.

"All right, now, where does it hurt?"

Dee put her hand to the back of her head. "Here."

"Do you feel dizzy?"

"A little bit." She did not look at Osei.

Mr. Brabant joined them. "Go to your class lines, everyone," he commanded, his authority so clear that the spell was broken and students began to move. "Not you," he added as O made to follow the others heading toward the school entrance. "What did you do, Osei?"

O was silent.

"He didn't do anything," Dee answered. "I—I ran up to him and tripped and fell, that's all."

Mimi started. "Dee, that's not—"

"It's not Osei's fault. He tried to catch me."

Mr. Brabant raised his eyebrows. "Really?"

"Really. I was clumsy. You know how clumsy I am."

"If you tripped you would have fallen forward, wouldn't you? Not backward. You've learned about momentum in class."

"I tripped," Dee insisted, struggling to her feet. "I'm fine. Really." She still did not look at Osei.

Mr. Brabant and Miss Lode glanced at each other. "All right," Mr. Brabant said. "Go to the nurse's office so she can check you over and get you an ice pack for that bump on your head. You go with her, Mimi. Look after her. And do something about her hair. Her mother will complain otherwise, and we'll never hear the end of it."

Osei kept his eyes on the ground rather than allowing his gaze to follow the girls as they left. He didn't dare look up. Dee's covering for him did not make things better, but worse. His anger had not abated, but solidified into a lump in his gut. It was not so much anger at her, but at himself. He had pushed a girl. You did not do that. His mother would be so horrified, she would not even shout or wail; she would turn away from him. Even Sisi, with all her righteous anger at white people, would not condone what Osei had done.

He could feel both sets of teachers' eyes on him as he stood, head bowed, awaiting their judgment.

"I've seen your kind before. You planning to be a troublemaker at this school, boy?" Mr. Brabant muttered.

"No, sir." The words came out of him like a reflex.

"Because we don't take kindly to such behavior here."

"No, sir."

"You're lucky you've got a girl who likes you enough to lie for you. God knows why."

Osei studied the asphalt—scene of many a scraped knee. He wondered why playgrounds weren't covered with more forgiving grass.

"I didn't expect much from a bl—" he glanced at Miss Lode. "From you. And I haven't been surprised today. But if anything else happens and you are anywhere nearby? The principal will expel you, no matter how much a pretty girl defends you. Do you hear me?"

Osei clenched his teeth until he thought they would break, and after a moment nodded.

"All right." Mr. Brabant raised his voice. "What are you all doing still standing here? Why aren't you in your lines? I'm counting to ten and you'd better be there or there will be detentions!"

Amid the students scurrying across the playground, the two teachers walked unhurriedly. Osei trudged behind; he couldn't face the indignity of running ahead of them to get in line, even if he got detention.

"Richard, I . . ." Miss Lode hesitated.

"What?" Mr. Brabant barked, as if he were talking to a student. "Sorry, Diane. What?"

"Well—I wonder if we're being a little hard on him."

"Hard on him? He just knocked a girl over!"

"Yes, but . . . this can't be easy for him, being all alone in the school."

"Life is not easy for anyone. If anything, he has it *too* easy. He'll grow up and walk right into a good job, thanks to affirmative action. A good job that someone more qualified should have done."

"Did that happen to— Never mind." Miss Lode sighed. "Lord, what is wrong today? First Casper, now this. Did they put something in the lunches?"

"You know why," Mr. Brabant answered darkly. "This school isn't ready for a black boy."

"I guess not."

"And the day isn't over yet. You know what they say: trouble always comes in threes."

❋

All traces of Mimi's headache had been scoured away, and everything had come back into sharp focus. It was as if she were looking through a pair of binoculars, turning and turning the knobs until they snapped into place and she could see clearly what had been a blur before.

Maybe it was because Ian was leaving her alone. Since Monday morning by the flagpole when she had agreed to be his girlfriend, she had felt his attention pressing on her like a heavy quilt pinning her to the bed. Even out of sight he somehow made his presence felt—either by the persistent attention his friend Rod paid her, keeping tabs on her for Ian, or by the way the playground functioned around him: the kids who followed him or feared him or ignored him running in distinct motions like a machine in which Ian was the center. Briefly Mimi had been pulled into that center with him, and it was so alien a place that she could barely function—as a student, as a girlfriend, as a friend. Buying her freedom from him with the strawberry pencil case had been worth it for the feeling she'd had during kickball that she was now insignificant. Ian's attention had shifted to others, and Mimi could breathe again, could close her eyes and find her own place far from scrutiny.

But she felt guilty: she knew instinctively that nothing good would come of Ian now being in possession of that case—and Osei's address and phone number. She regretted not thinking to remove the piece of paper before handing it over. Most of all she felt guilty for betraying Dee by giving away something precious of hers. It was disloyal.

She sighed. *At least I can help Dee now—that's something,* she thought as she linked her arm through her friend's and walked her upstairs to see the nurse.

Miss Montano's office on the second floor was a small box of a room, with a bathroom attached and the transistor radio permanently tuned to WPGC, the local Top 40 station. They had all been there before to see Miss Montano for cuts and stomachaches and fevers. Mimi was a regular with her headaches. The door was ajar, and over the sound of "Band on the Run" on the radio, Mimi could hear whimpers and the nurse's admonishment to "stop being a baby."

She and Dee sat down to wait in a row of chairs set out in the hall. Across from them, posters had been taped to the wall. A reminder to wash your hands after using the bathroom. How to deal with hair lice. The signs for chicken pox, mumps, measles. Posters about having a TB test, an eye test, a shot for smallpox or polio. Just sitting across from all this adult information exhausted her. They were good at making the world into a fearful place. For a second she wished her mother were sitting with them, to take over the burden of worry.

More yelps were heard from the office. A scraped knee, Mimi predicted, which Miss Montano would be cleaning with iodine. Probably a young student, a second or third grader. She had sat here so many times that she had heard it all before.

Dee was leaning back, eyes closed. Mimi wanted to ask how she was doing; in fact, there were many things she wanted to ask, and to say. But she knew from experience with headaches that fussing didn't help. Instead she tried to be practical. "I'm going to get some water. Do you want some?"

"Yes, please."

Mimi pulled two Dixie Riddle Cups from a dispenser on the wall and went to the water fountain down the hall to fill them. When she got back, "Reelin' in the Years" by Steely Dan was playing and Dee was crying. Mimi sat down and handed her the cup. "Drink."

Dee drank in one gulp, then crushed the paper cup without reading her riddle. Mimi sipped hers, glancing at the joke on the side of the cup. *What does a mirror do when you tell it a joke? It cracks up.* They were never funny.

"Right," she said. "I'm going to rebraid your hair. One braid or two?"

"One."

"French braid?"

"French. No—normal. Make it simple."

"Turn your back."

Dee turned away from Mimi, who sat sideways in her seat and pulled her friend's hair over her shoulders. She began combing the thick blond tresses with her fingers to calm and tame them. She had rarely seen Dee's hair free from braids. It seemed a shame to confine it again. Still, it clearly bothered the adults.

Mimi divided Dee's hair into three. "Now, tell me what's wrong," she said as she began weaving the strands in and out.

"Oh . . ." Dee shook her head. "It's nothing."

"It's not nothing. What happened out there?" Mimi had been sitting with her eyes closed, willing herself far from the playground, and had only caught the end of Dee's fall, the smack of her head against the ground, but she'd seen the ugly fury in Osei's face and knew Dee could not have tripped as she'd claimed.

"I don't know why he's mad at me." Dee wiped her eyes with a hand. "I don't know what I've done. Everything was so great, and then . . . suddenly it wasn't. It's like a switch has been flipped, like someone said something to him about me. But what would anyone say? I haven't done anything wrong! Except . . ."

"What?"

Dee shook her head. "Nothing."

When it became clear she would not elaborate, Mimi shook her own head. "Boys are strange."

"Are you and Ian—"

"We just broke up." Mimi thought of the exchange—strawberry case for breakup—and a pang of guilt twisted her stomach. She should tell Dee. Did she have the nerve to?

Dee turned to look at Mimi. "Oh! That's—" She appeared to gulp back a word, but she seemed relieved—which hurt Mimi more than she'd expected. Clearly her judgment had been in question, even if Dee hadn't said anything about it these past few days.

"That's good," Mimi filled in. "I know. I don't know what got into me to go with him in the first place."

"Well . . ." Dee smiled for the first time. "We kind of wondered. He's so different from you."

"I guess I was flattered. No boy has wanted to go with me before. Because I'm weird."

"No, you're not!"

"Yes, I am. You know I am. I've always been on the sidelines. I'm not very good at anything. I don't get good grades, I can't run fast, I can't draw or write or sing. I get these silly headaches. Everyone thinks I'm a witch or something. Sometimes I'm amazed that I'm your best friend." *Especially when I give your things away and lie to you,* she added silently.

"Don't be silly, you're the most interesting person I know—apart from Osei, now."

Mimi felt the sharp tooth of jealousy bite, and was tempted to yank hard on the braid she held. Instead she reeled herself in and, giving the braid only a gentle tug, she announced, "There. Do you have a ponytail holder?"

Dee dug into her jeans pocket. "You're also very good at turning Double-Dutch ropes," she said, handing Mimi a purple elastic.

Mimi wasn't sure how serious Dee was and decided it must be a joke. She laughed. "Yes, I am good at that." She dropped the braid. "Done."

"Thanks." Dee leaned her head back against the wall, then winced and shifted to rest her cheek against her hand. "Hurts."

"The bump?"

"Yeah."

"You hit it pretty hard. Do you feel dizzy or sick?"

"No."

"Good. That probably means you don't have a concussion. That's what the nurse will be worried about."

They were silent. Now was the moment when Mimi should confess to her friend about the pencil case. She swallowed, opened her mouth—but nothing came out. It was so hard to admit to bad behavior. And with her hair back in a braid, Dee looked calmer, more herself. Mimi was reluctant to upset her.

Then another song came on, and the moment was gone. Mimi and Dee sat up.

> I heard he sang a good song
> I heard he had a style
> And so I came to see him
> To listen for a while

Even the tinniness of the radio couldn't disguise Roberta Flack's rich voice. The girls had been crazy about the song ever since it came out over a year ago. A fifth grade girl with a strong voice had won the school's talent show this year with it, though Mimi had overheard Mr. Brabant mutter to Miss Lode that it was a wholly inappropriate song for a ten-year-old to sing. Dee began to hum along.

> Strumming my pain with his fingers
> Singing my life with his words
> Killing me softly with his song...

She broke off. "Oh, Mimi, I don't know what to do."

"Do you like Osei?"

"Yes. A lot. It felt so good being with him. He's so different from anyone else here."

Mimi was silent, trying not to take it as a criticism.

"He's been so many places and has things to say. He makes everyone else seem boring. And me boring too, living in this boring suburb. It makes me want to do more adventurous things, like go downtown more often. When was the last time you went into DC?"

"Easter—we took my cousins up the Washington Monument."

"I was going to ask Osei to take the bus with me this weekend—to Georgetown, maybe."

"What about your mother?"

"What about her?" The defiance Dee had displayed earlier with Mr. Brabant was rearing up again.

"Never mind. You can say you're with me if you want."

"I won't need to if he stays mad at me. I feel like we have to make up or break up."

"Did he push you just now?"

Dee didn't answer.

"'Cause if he did, that's bad, isn't it?"

"It was an accident. He didn't mean to hurt me, I'm sure."

"Are you?"

"I'm more worried about how he acted with me before that, during the kickball game, and even before that. Why did he change so fast? Seem to care, then suddenly so angry and distant?"

Mimi shrugged. "I don't understand boys. And they don't understand us."

"Ow!" they heard inside; then, "Jimmy, I'm almost done. Sit still!"

> He sang as if he knew me
> In all my dark despair
> And then he looked right through me
> As if I wasn't there

Dee was crying again. Mimi knew it was best to leave her alone.

Maybe she could get the strawberry case back from Ian before he did anything with it—sold it or whatever he was planning. She would steel herself and ask him.

There were scuffles in the office, and Dee managed to wipe her eyes before the door swung wide and a young boy limped out, patched up on his knee and elbow, followed by Miss Montano, who wore a white coat and a face set permanently to unperturbed.

"Back you go to class, Jimmy," she said. "Next time look where you're going. Honestly—boys," she muttered, before turning to Mimi and Dee. "All right, then, girls. Another headache, Mimi?"

"No, Miss Montano, I'm just accompanying Dee. Miss Lode asked me to. She's bumped her head."

"Have you? Dee, come in and I'll look you over." She nodded at Mimi. "You can go back to class. If nothing's wrong, Dee can see herself back. If she's hurt herself, I'll send her home." Miss Montano's briskness was comforting, as responsibility was deftly removed from Mimi. Let the adults take charge.

She squeezed Dee's hand. "See you later."

Dee nodded and rose to follow the nurse inside. "Thanks, Mimi."

"Sure."

Mimi remained seated after they had gone inside, waiting for Roberta to finish singing out her pain, wondering what the next song would be and if it would provide a sign. She didn't tell Dee and the others, but she looked for signs in things sometimes if she was confused. Her brain was fizzing now; she needed to feed it with knowledge that would make sense of the day.

When Dr. John began to sing about being in the right place at the wrong time, Mimi nodded. The sign made sense to her: this whole day felt like the wrong time. She couldn't wait for it to be over.

PART V

AFTER SCHOOL

My mommy told me
If I was goody
That she would buy me
A rubber dolly

My sister told her
I kissed a soldier
Now she won't buy me
That rubber dolly

Now I am dead
And in my grave
And there beside me
A rubber dolly

Dee was relieved when the bell rang for the end of school. She felt as if she'd been waiting for it for hours. When she'd returned from the nurse, having missed the grammar test, Osei did not smile when she sat down, and he ignored her for what was left of the afternoon. She could feel the ice on him as they sat side by side during Art, making Mother's Day cards from construction paper, magazines, tissue paper, glitter, pipe cleaners, and other materials distributed to the desk clusters. It was particularly painful when someone was sitting right next to you as they froze you out.

Art was class time Dee had always looked forward to, when Mr. Brabant stepped out and Mrs. Randolph took over and everything became softer and less rigid. You could talk to your friends while your hands were busy. Mrs. Randolph encouraged it. "We create best when we are relaxed and free," she said, waving her hands so that her myriad bangles jingled. She always wore bright red lipstick that bled over her lips into the web of tiny wrinkles surrounding them. "Light. And passion. That is what we're looking for. *Comme les Français.*" Mrs. Randolph had been to Paris several times and liked to remind the students by sprinkling French throughout her pep talks.

She wanted them to make unusual cards for their mothers, not just a drawing of flowers with "Happy Mother's Day, Mom" printed inside. "Look at all these things you can use for your cards," she said. "Feel them." She threw the tissue paper in the air, riffled through magazines, waved vials of silver glitter. "Be inspired. Think about your mother and all that she does for you," she added as the students looked blank. "How much she loves you and how much she has sacrificed for your happiness. Express the love you have for her on this piece of paper." She held one of the white cards she had distributed. "Express yourself and honor your mother. *Ah, l'amour pour la mère, c'est merveilleux!*"

Dee giggled nervously and glanced sideways at O. He did not look up. His face was stern, his eyes glued to his card. Dee bit her lip and looked across at Patty, who pouted sympathetically. "How's your head?" she asked pointedly, frowning at O, as if to remind Dee that she should be angry at him.

Next to her, Osei flinched.

It was a timely reminder. She *should* be angry—she had a right to be. He had pushed her, hurt her unfairly. He should be saying he was sorry. She should be glaring at him, insisting on changing seats so she didn't have to sit with him—maybe move across to Casper's empty seat at the next cluster. Other girls would do that. Blanca would be noisy with it, and enjoy the fuss she could legitimately make.

Yet Dee did not feel angry, but guilty—like she should be apologizing to him rather than the other way around. He had a right to be angry at her, she felt, to shout and push her away. He was black, and all day they had treated him that way, differently from how they would treat another new student. Dee knew she herself found him interesting because he was black, and that was not necessarily a good reason—to like someone for their skin color. She watched his hands now, the brown of her dad's morning coffee, using scissors to cut out a shape from red construction paper that looked like a lopsided heart. His fingernails were long and square and very pink.

"Dee?"

Patty was staring at her, and Dee jumped. "I'm fine. My head is all right." She quickly picked up a blue pipe cleaner without knowing what to do with it.

"Who do we have here?" Mrs. Randolph had fluttered over to their desks. "You must be new. I'm sure I would have remembered you otherwise!" She smiled down at O. There was lipstick on her large front teeth.

Osei stopped cutting but did not look up. "Yes, ma'am."

Mrs. Randolph laughed. "Oh, no need to be formal with me! What's your name?"

"Osei."

"What an interesting name! Well, Osei, you can call me Kay." Mrs. Randolph was always trying to get the students to call her by her first name. No one ever did. "There is no hierarchy here. There never is in art. There is just expression. And today we are expressing our love and respect for our mothers. What are you making for your card to her?"

Dee wanted to tell him not to worry, that Mrs. Randolph paid this sort of embarrassing attention to everyone at some point. You just had to grit your teeth and let it wash over you, then once she'd moved on you could sit back and laugh at her behind her back. But of course Dee couldn't say such a thing, not with him so clearly shutting her out.

He looked up at Mrs. Randolph and said, "I am cutting out strawberries for her. They are her favorite fruit."

Dee's stomach curdled. Mrs. Randolph clapped her hands. "*Formidable!* Choosing something specific to her—that's wonderful! Now, don't be constrained by the materials here. You don't even have to use scissors if you don't want to. You can tear out the strawberries from the paper if you like! Do you want to tear them out?" Clean lines seemed to bother Mrs. Randolph much more than messiness.

Osei looked down and began cutting again. "I am using scissors."

"Of course, of course!" Mrs. Randolph shrilled nervously. "*Super!* Now, Dee, what are you doing? How will you celebrate your mother?"

"I—I—" Dee fiddled with the pipe cleaner she held, curling it in on itself so that it became a fuzzy circle. She had no idea what to make for her mother. Mrs. Benedetti was not the sort of mother you "celebrated."

"Blueberries!" Mrs. Randolph cried. "Is that *your* mother's favorite fruit? Maybe this will be the fruit table. Osei, you are setting a trend!" She gazed expectantly at Duncan's and Patty's cards, hoping perhaps to see bananas depicted, or oranges. But Duncan was asleep with his head on his arms; while Mr. Brabant would never have allowed Duncan to sleep in class, Mrs. Randolph was more lenient. Patty was painstakingly constructing a tissue-paper flower that the girls had learned to make the year before with another, more traditional art teacher. For a moment Mrs. Randolph looked as if she wanted to pluck the flower from Patty and rip it up. Instead she smiled brightly and turned to another cluster of desks. "And what will we find here? Favorite vegetables?" She let loose her crashing laugh and Dee winced.

If Duncan were awake and it were the beginning of the day, when she and Osei were still happy together, the four of them—even prissy Patty—could have made fun of Mrs. Randolph—their imitations of her voice and recitations of her words lasting for days and becoming inside jokes. Instead they said nothing, but worked doggedly on their cards while all around them Dee heard her classmates having lighthearted fun.

Patty asked for a bathroom pass, and didn't come back to her own desk on her return, but lingered with friends across the classroom, comparing flowers and avoiding her grim cluster. Dee wanted to beg her to rejoin them, or kick Duncan awake, just to have a buffer of other students between her and Osei. Instead they had to sit stiffly, pretending each other wasn't there.

From the corner of her eye she watched his card take shape—a cluster of three strawberries glued to the front, the white card colored the same pink as the pencil case. Inside he wrote very formally, in handwriting that looked European, with long full loops on the Hs and Ps and Ys: "Dear Mother, I am wishing you a very happy Mother's Day, from your son, Osei."

Was that what his anger was about—the pencil case? Dee wondered where it was. She'd surreptitiously checked inside her desk on returning from the nurse, hoping that somehow it had reappeared, but it wasn't there. Though Osei hadn't turned his head, she felt sure he'd know what she was searching for. Had she dropped it somewhere? She would have to check Lost and Found.

Ten minutes before the end of school, Mrs. Randolph clapped her hands and asked the students to leave the cards they had made on their desks and walk around looking at everyone else's before starting to clean up. Dee jumped up, relieved. The last half hour had felt like punishment for a crime she did not know she had committed. And she had ended up making a stupid card with blueberries on the front, when her mother didn't even eat blueberries. It looked like she was copying Osei's card.

He too seemed eager to get away from their cluster of desks. As she walked around admiring the tissue-paper flowers and drawings of flowers and a few pieces of fruit (but no vegetables), Dee found herself hyperaware of where he was in relation to her. Soon he seemed to disappear altogether, until eventually she found him in the reading corner, sitting on a beanbag and flipping through a *Mad* magazine someone had left there.

"Osei, we have to clean up now, before the bell rings."

He merely nodded, then got up and slouched toward their desks. Dee recalled how confidently he had walked across the playground that morning. Where had that confidence gone?

As they worked together, dumping paper and crayons and bottles of Elmer's glue and pipe cleaners into a cardboard box, Osei said in a low voice, "Meet me on the playground after school."

Dee nodded miserably. Her mother was expecting her home, but she would tell her she'd stayed after to jump rope.

When the bell rang, she murmured, "I'll be there in a minute." Then she hurried out of the classroom and down the hall to Lost and Found, which was in a box outside the principal's office.

As she knelt to rummage through what seemed to be a tangle of the same blue cardigans, interspersed with single sneakers, Dee could hear Mrs. Duke on the phone: "No, he hasn't actually done anything wrong. Not anything punishable. But he was involved in an incident with a girl—no, not that kind of thing, she fell and bumped her head." Pause. "I simply wanted to make you aware of it." Pause. "I understand that. Of course it can take time to settle in to a new school, especially for someone of your son's ... circumstances. He may not be used to behaving in the ways we expect of our children." Pause. "No, I'm not implying—" Pause. "Of course. I am not suggesting you have not done your job. Let's just give him time to settle in, shall we? We will keep an eye on him." Pause. "That won't be necessary. Give it a couple weeks, Mrs. Kokote, and we'll speak again, all right? Now, I'm afraid the bell has rung and I have a staff meeting. Goodbye." When she'd hung up she muttered, "Lord, give me strength!"

The school secretary who worked in the adjacent office chuckled. "Giving you a hard time, was she?"

"Uppity, is what I'd call it. Thank God we only have him for a month. Let the next school deal with him."

"You think he pushed Dee Benedetti?"

Dee froze. If she moved, the secretary would see her.

"I *know* he did. Several of the children told me they saw him do it. But Dee won't say he did, and that makes any accusations awkward."

"What, he's turned her head, has he? Given her a taste for chocolate milk?"

Mrs. Duke grunted. "So to speak."

"It won't last. These kids get together at recess and break up at lunchtime. It's the age."

"I don't know. Diane told me Dee had taken her braids out and let him touch her hair. Her mother won't be pleased. I'm dreading making that phone call. You know what Mrs. Benedetti's like."

"Oh yes." The secretary laughed again. "Dee hasn't actually broken a rule, though, has she? So you don't have to call her mother."

"I do, to tell her about the bump to her head. But all I have to say is that she tripped. I don't have to bring up the boy, thank God. Never mind. I expect I'll catch him out eventually, Dee or no Dee."

Then the secretary looked up and saw her hanging over the Lost and Found box. "Dee, what are you doing there?"

"Nothing! Just looking for something. It's not here."
As Dee got to her feet she heard a chair scrape, and
footsteps, then Mrs. Duke appeared in the doorway,
her perfume preceding her. She seemed startled.

"Dee, have you been eavesdropping?"

"No, Mrs. Duke. I was looking for something in Lost
and Found."

"What were you looking for?"

"A—a pencil case." Dee found it impossible to look
her in the eye, so kept focused on her pearl necklace.
Mrs. Duke alternated it with a spider brooch or, during the winter, a snowflake brooch studded with rhine-
stones. Dee and her friends called her "Spidey," "Flakey,"
or "Pearly," depending on which she was wearing.

"What does it look like?"

"It's pink, with strawberries on it. But it's not here.
It's . . . lost."

"Right. Off you go, then."

Dee hurried away, but stopped when Mrs. Duke
called after her, "Wait a minute."

She turned. "Yes, Mrs. Duke?"

The principal folded her arms over her chest as
adults often did when they talked to children. "How's
your head?"

"It's OK."

"I am concerned about you, Dee. Concerned that you
may not be telling the whole truth about what happened this afternoon."

Dee scowled. "I *am* telling the truth. I tripped and
fell."

"Are you sure?"

"Yes."

Mrs. Duke held her gaze for a long moment, during which Dee pressed her mouth tight and stuck out her chin. At last the principal turned away. "All right. That's what I will tell your mother," she said over her shoulder. "I'm going to call her now. You go home."

As she walked down the hallway, Dee shuddered at what her mother would say if she knew what had really happened today. At the exit she paused. Osei was waiting by the jungle gym. She took a deep breath and stepped outside.

✳

Ian never went home right away unless it was raining. There was nothing to do at home. His older brothers didn't arrive back till later, and anyway they were not interested in doing things with him. When he went out into the neighborhood, to shoot hoops or throw a baseball or play kick the can, he'd noticed that after his arrival the other kids would find excuses to leave, saying they had homework or their mothers needed them to go to the store. One time Ian had ridden his bike around and discovered the same boys who'd left the local park ten minutes before had reconvened in a vacant lot to continue their softball game without him. He had hidden, too humiliated to let them see him. But he'd placed each name on a mental list and systematically gone through it, punishing them over the next few weeks. Not with his usual bullying: squeezing out money or physically hurting them or making his presence felt. Instead he was stealthier, meaner—slashing bicycle tires, touching a sister in a crowd, dumping paint in a desk during recess.

He preferred to remain on the playground after school. Though many children left to go home, it was open for an hour for those who wanted to stay and play, with one of the teachers as a monitor. Today it was Miss Lode. That was good—she was too scared of him to interfere much. At the moment she was talking to the parent of a younger student from the other playground. Soon she would sit and read a book, glancing up now and then.

Ian spotted O by the jungle gym—a frame of metal bars bolted together at right angles to make box shapes up to a height of twelve feet, which could be climbed all over. There were a few other students around, but none on the jungle gym. Maybe they were avoiding the new boy.

Ian took his time to make his way over. There was no need to rush; that would be undignified. Instead he paused briefly by the girls jumping their inevitable Double Dutch, a mix of grades now. Mimi was with them, turning for a fourth grader who jumped as the other girls sang:

> My mommy told me
> If I was goody
> That she would buy me
> A rubber dolly
>
> My sister told her
> I kissed a soldier
> Now she won't buy me
> That rubber dolly

He didn't stay any longer to watch—she was too young to have breasts that bounced when she jumped. As he left they were still singing:

> Now I am dead
> And in my grave
> And there beside me
> A rubber dolly

Ian went on to a group of boys playing marbles, standing so that his shadow fell across the circle. The boys looked up, annoyed and ready to complain, but said nothing when they realized whose shadow it was. Ian remained just long enough for the shooter to miss before he moved on.

He had not yet reached the jungle gym when Rod caught up with him, his black eye even more prominent after a few hours of swelling. Rod was seriously getting on his nerves—had been even before today. Didn't he need to fight his own battles, win his own girls? Hadn't he learned enough from Ian to do so on his own? He had been the sidekick for too long, and Ian preferred to go it alone now.

"Man, I don't understand something," Rod began. When Ian kept walking, Rod ran ahead and stood in front of him to make him stop. Anger flared, but Ian pulled back from slamming a hand into Rod's chest. Rod was not important; he should save his actions for someone else.

"You promised I would go with Dee," Rod continued, whining. "But now I don't know who my competition is. Is it him or him?" He waved one skinny arm at O by the jungle gym, and the other at Casper, lurking over by the entrance to the school gym, out of sight of Miss Lode. Ian smiled to himself: Casper the golden boy, belatedly discovering how to break the rules. He had been suspended; he should be across the street now, getting punished by his parents—being grounded and having his allowance docked, as his parents were unlikely to use the belt he deserved. Instead he had come back to school and was probably waiting for Blanca. Now that he'd had a taste of bad behavior, he was indulging in it.

"I don't even understand why I picked that fight with Casper," Rod added. "He's going with Blanca—anybody can see that. You saw them kissing at recess. Why'd you have me go after him? It's *him*"—he waved again at O, who frowned—"who's going with Dee. And he hurt her! I should be fighting *him*." He clenched his fists in a show of bravery, but it didn't conceal his fear as he contemplated his rival. "I don't know, though—I might get hurt even worse than with Casper."

"You probably would," Ian agreed. "But don't worry— I think it's all gonna change soon. Just hang on a little longer. And leave O to me." He began walking again toward the jungle gym but stopped, putting his palm out to halt Rod as he made to follow him. "Just me." Rod dropped back, an injured animal left behind. Ian was going to have to find a way to shake him loose. Tomorrow. Today he had another target.

O had been watching him. When Ian joined him at the jungle gym he said, "What did *he* want?"

Ian sat down on one of the metal bars and rested his

hands on the ones on either side. "Rod? Nothing. He's nothing."

O had his eyes on Rod, now mooching toward the pirate ship. "It does not seem like nothing. What does he want with me?"

Ian let himself sag into the boxy frame. "Rod likes Dee. So he's jealous. The green-eyed monster, my father calls it. And"—Ian calculated for a moment, then decided to try it—"Dee likes him too."

O stiffened, his eyes wild. "What? Him too?!"

Ian smiled to himself. O was in such a state that he'd believe anything—even that a scrawny nothing of a boy like Rod could catch Dee's eye. "Looks like you picked the wrong girl. I could've told you that."

O crossed his arms over his chest and tucked his hands under his armpits. He seemed to be trying to contain his anger. "She picked me." He paused. "She is meeting me here in a minute. I was ready to tell her that it is OK, I am not angry anymore. But I cannot trust her, can I?" He looked at Ian as if he wanted a reminder of the evidence.

So Ian provided it. "The pencil case, remember? How did Casper get it?"

Even as he said it he knew that the power of the case was only going to last as long as no one asked questions. Once O or Dee asked Casper or Blanca about where the case came from, Ian's involvement would be uncovered. That was the flaw in his strategy—he was likely to be pulled into it. The damage had to be done now—enough damage that afterward it wouldn't matter what part Ian had played.

At that moment Blanca ran out of the building and around the corner to where Casper was waiting for her by the gym. As they embraced, Blanca let her backpack drop. The strawberry case, stuffed into the open front pocket, was just visible.

"What did Dee say about the case when you asked her?"

O's face fell. "She said it was at home."

"So"—Ian nodded toward Blanca and the case—"why is Dee lying to you, then? Is it because she thinks it doesn't matter if she lies to you because you won't get it? Because you're stupid?"

He didn't add "because you're black." He didn't need to—O had reached that point all by himself. His whole being seemed to hollow out, like a sandcastle at the beach collapsing in on itself. "Do not say that."

"I'm just being honest. Dee's usually a nice girl. I'm trying to figure out what she's up to, and why. She's not used to black people, see. So maybe she's trying you out like a new flavor of ice cream."

O closed his eyes.

Enough, Ian thought. *I've said enough. Perfect timing too.*

"Here comes Dee," he said. "I'll leave you guys alone."

＊

In the past when kids had said or done things—left bananas on his desk or made hooting noises like monkeys or whispered to each other that he smelled different or asked him if his grandparents had been slaves—Osei had preserved enough distance to cushion himself from the blow so that it didn't hurt. Often he could even laugh it off—repeat it to Sisi later, make fun of the ignorance or lack of creativity in their prejudice. "Can they not think up something more original than a monkey?" he'd say to his sister. "Why don't they ever call me a panther? It is darker than a monkey."

Sisi had chuckled. "'Cause honkies are scared of Black Panthers." She raised her fist in the salute.

In some ways overt racism based on ignorance was easier to deal with. It was the more subtle digs that got to him. The kids who were friendly at school but didn't ask him to their birthday parties even when they had invited the rest of the class. The conversations that stopped when he walked into a room, a slight pause reserved for his presence. The remarks made and then the addendum, "Oh, I don't mean you, Osei. You're different." Or a comment like "he's black but he's smart," and the inability to understand why that was offensive. The assumption that he was better at sports because black people just—you know—*are*, or at dancing, or at committing crimes. The way people talked about Africa as if it were just one country. The inability to tell black people apart, so Muhammad Ali and Joe Frazier were mixed up, or Tina Turner and Aretha Franklin, or Flip Wilson and Bill Cosby—though none of them looked anything like the other.

He was angrier at himself than at Dee. For a brief time—a morning—he had let his guard down, allowed himself to think she was different, that she liked him for himself rather than for what he represented—a black boy, exotic, other; an unknown territory to be explored. He watched her walking toward him on the playground now and felt his emotions zigzag between sorrow, anger, and pity. If he ignored what Ian said, he could feel something more positive: gratitude for her attention, physical attraction, interest in her interest in him. But how could he ignore the strawberry case? The lie that changed everything. He had opened himself up to Dee and already she couldn't be trusted. Suddenly he wished Sisi were at home and he could say to her, "Why does being black have to hurt so much?"

"Go back to Africa, little brother," she would answer, "where being black is normal and white skin is made fun of." It was tempting. His parents would probably love it if he asked to go to boarding school in Ghana.

"Hey," Dee said as she reached his side, hesitant, fearful.

O twisted his mouth into an ugly smirk. "Where were you?" he demanded, sounding more imperious than he felt.

"Nowhere. I was just ... looking for something in Lost and Found." Dee was reluctant, and shifty, and miserable.

"What did you lose?"

There was a pause that told him all he needed to know as he watched her trying to think of something, her face transparent. Another lie was about to join the first.

"A—a sweater. I think I left it on the ground when I was jumping Double Dutch the other day."

"Did you find it?"

"No."

"Maybe you left it at home."

Dee was silent.

"Are you sure you were not looking for something else?"

Dee froze. "What do you mean?"

Osei nodded over at Blanca and Casper by the gym. She was sitting in his lap, her arms around his neck, talking and laughing, and O felt the sharp lance of envy at their happiness pierce him.

"What about them?"

"Look at Blanca's backpack."

Dee squinted. "I don't know what I'm supposed to see."

It was hard to spot it from where they were, unless you knew what you were looking for. "Climb to the top—you will see better from there." Osei began pulling himself up the bars of the jungle gym.

Dee hesitated below. "Why don't you just tell me what to look for?"

"Come up," Osei insisted.

She still stood there, reluctant.

"Dee, if you do not come up here ..."

Dee began to climb, slow and careful, until she reached the top, where she sat on one of the metal bars and held tight to two others. "I got stuck up here once in fourth grade. Mr. Brabant had to carry me down." She looked expectant, then disappointed when Osei didn't say anything. "So it's a big deal that I've come up here for you," she added. "What did you want me to see?"

"There. Look at what is in the pocket of Blanca's backpack. Is that what you have been searching for?"

Dee looked for a long moment, then gripped the bars even tighter. "How did that get there?"

"You told me you left it at home during lunch."

"I thought I had."

"Did you—really?"

Dee sighed. "I didn't know where it was."

"So you lied to me."

"I—I thought I would find it—that I left it somewhere and would find it. I didn't want to upset you by telling you I didn't know where it was."

"So that is what you were looking for in Lost and Found."

Dee nodded. "I know it was your sister's and you wouldn't like it if I lost it. I was trying to find it so you didn't ever need to know it was lost."

For a brief moment Osei believed her. He wanted to, and she seemed sincere, and sorry. Then from the corner of his eye he caught a movement—Ian was sitting on the pirate ship with Rod; they were dangling their legs over the side, swinging them back and forth.

"Or so you say," he persisted.

"I was!"

"How did Blanca get the case, then?"

"I have no idea. Let's ask her."

"I do not need to—I already know. She got it from Casper, who you gave it to. You gave my sister's pencil case to another boy."

"No! Why would I give it to Casper?"

"I do not know. Why *would* you give it to Casper?"

She looked at him, puzzled, with a flash of anger directed at his cheap trick of throwing her words back at her. If he weren't so angry he would be embarrassed at himself.

"You are two-timing me, aren't you? You are going with Casper."

"What?!"

"You probably already were before today. Probably everybody knows and thinks it is so funny how you are lying to the black boy." He looked around the playground, which had turned into a battleground, with many enemies.

"Osei, no!"

"Ian is the only one with the decency to be honest with me. At least he told me what is really happening."

"Ian? What's he—" Dee's face shifted from incredulity to a sudden understanding. She shook her head. "You know you shouldn't always believe what Ian says. He says what he does for his own gain."

"Do not try to defend yourself by putting down others."

"But ..." Dee made a visible effort to gather herself together. "Osei, I have never gone with Casper," she said carefully. "I've known him all my life, but I don't feel like that about him the way I do—I did—do about you. And look"—she gestured toward Casper and Blanca—"you can see for yourself he's with Blanca."

O listened to her stumble over her tenses and left a silence before he spoke. "Why did you keep talking about him to me so much?"

"Because he could be a good friend to you. He could help you. Ian said—" She stopped.

"Ian said what?"

But Dee was staring over at the pirate ship, where Ian and Rod were casually tossing pebbles at the boys playing marbles.

The rage surged in Osei again, so angry her attention was straying from what was important that he wanted to shake her. He began to reach across to grab her arm, but Dee was already stepping down to the lower rung so that she was just out of reach. "Dee," he said.

She kept climbing down, and when she reached the ground she began striding toward Ian on the ship.

"Do not walk away from me, Dee!" he shouted.

His tone made the boys look up from their marbles and the girls stop jumping Double Dutch. He had all of their attention, though he had not asked for it. But now that he had it, he could use it to punish her.

"Do not walk away," he repeated, raising his voice. Then he added a word he had heard before but never imagined he would ever use, or know how to use: "Whore!"

The word cracked across the playground like thunder. Anyone who hadn't been listening did now. Even Blanca and Casper surfaced from making out to look around.

Dee stopped, one foot frozen behind her, her single braid an emphatic line down her back. Rod jumped up from the ship deck, but Ian restrained him.

Across the playground Miss Lode dropped her book. "Did I hear—" She looked puzzled, and embarrassed too, as the children turned to stare at her. She gulped, bowed her head, and picked up the book.

"You know that this girl is a whore?" O hissed,

directing his words at his audience: the boys with their marbles, the jump-rope girls, Casper and Blanca, Ian and Rod. It felt powerful, having the right kind of attention at last. He smiled, exposing his side teeth; he looked like a wolf growling. "You know she said she would go all the way with me," he continued, his voice rising again, "the way she already has with Casper!"

There was a gasp from Blanca, who jumped up from Casper's lap as he began shaking his head.

Dee turned around slowly, eyes huge, mouth open and trembling, and stared up at Osei at the top of the jungle gym. She held her hands out, palms up. "Why are you saying that?" she cried.

Guilt flicked through him, but the power of speaking and being heard at last was stronger, and took him over so that O hardly understood what he said now. "She has even touched my dick, that is how much she wants it. How much all white girls want it."

The marble boys shouted, then burst into nervous laughter. There was a collective gasp from the jump-rope girls, and Dee's eyes darted to them, her tribe. They were clearly shocked, some putting their hands over their mouths, others turning to whisper to their neighbors. Then they began to titter—apart from Mimi, who was shaking her head as if to shoo away a persistent bee.

That was when Dee crumbled. With a shriek she turned and ran, faster than O could have imagined, her feet slapping across the asphalt. Fumbling with the gate that opened onto the street, she got it open at last, ran through, and slammed it behind her. As she disappeared around the corner, Rod jumped off the ship and stumbled after her, though Dee had too much of a head start for him to catch up, and he soon turned back.

When she was gone the playground changed, as if the sun were cloaked by a cloud. The children on the playground began talking at once.

"Jesus H. Christ. First Casper, then Dee. What's going on today?"

"Can you believe he said that?"

"I can believe it."

"No!"

"I wouldn't mind if she touched *my* dick."

"Shut up!"

"No, you shut up."

"Poor Dee!"

"Dee wouldn't do such a thing. Would she?"

"I don't know. She had her hands all over him this morning."

"And she kissed him at lunch—did you see?"

"What were they doing over there in the sandpit, anyway?"

"She's kind of slutty. I've always thought so."

"Yeah."

Mimi was standing among the jump-rope girls, glaring at Osei. Blanca had crossed her arms over her chest and was shouting at Casper. Miss Lode was no longer reading, but standing uncertainly. In the midst of the tumult, Ian continued to lounge on the ship, smiling.

How am I ever going to explain this to Sisi? Osei thought. She would know what to say to all these white people. "Black is beautiful," he murmured. Never had he wanted to believe it more.

He wished he could put his head on his sister's shoulder now and cry.

✳

As she stared at Osei, Mimi experienced déjà vu, that curious feeling of having already lived through something. The sensation was more the feeling of familiarity, as well as a disconnection from the flow of reality. Sometimes Mimi got déjà vu several times a day, and it began to seem as if she were juddering through dreams interspersed with shafts of reality. Now she felt she had already experienced Dee's humiliation and the new boy's misplaced triumph on top of the jungle gym—though of course she hadn't. Dee had never been humiliated before, Osei never triumphant.

She rubbed her face to clear it of the scene she had just witnessed, then walked over to the jungle gym. From the corner of her eye she registered Ian scrambling down from the ship, and knew she didn't have long.

"Osei, why did you lie?" she called up to him. "You know it's not true."

O gazed down at her from his perch as newly crowned king of the jungle gym. "I know what I know," he answered. "I have proof."

"What proof? It better be good for you to say that about Dee."

"Come up and you can see the proof for yourself." O gestured toward the corner of the playground by the gym.

Mimi frowned, wondering what he meant but concerned she might see actual evidence that he was right.

She couldn't bear that. She had been best friends with Dee nearly all her life; she did not want to discover that she didn't know her friend at all.

But curiosity, and the sense of Ian bearing down on her, made her climb. Mimi had only gotten six feet off the ground and was saying to O, "What am I looking for?" when she felt hands grab her ankle and then a sharp tug that dislodged her from the bars of the jungle gym. She was only in the air for a brief moment before landing hard on her neck, and the jolt of pain that flooded her body was so overwhelming she didn't even feel her head bang against the asphalt. Stars burst and swam before her eyes like tadpoles, and she blacked out for a moment.

When Mimi came to, her head hurt, much worse and more focused than any headache. She lay still, barely breathing. The pain was so acute that she couldn't even yell or cry, but hoped it would wash through her and recede like the tide. Then she opened her eyes and Ian was standing over her, his face flat, shaking his head with the tiniest of movements, a gesture meant just for her. Hanging over him like a dark moon, high above on the jungle gym, was Osei's worried face. "Are you OK, Mimi?" he called.

Then Blanca was pushing Ian aside and kneeling by her, her backpack dropping off her shoulder and landing near Mimi. "Oh my God, Mimi!" she cried, cupping her cheeks. "Are you dead?" At the same time Casper was shoving Ian away and saying, "What the hell did you do that for?"

Mimi's eyes slid to the backpack and the strawberry case stuffed in the outside pocket. She tuned out the buzzing and the yelling so that she could focus on those strawberries so close to her face. She was relieved to see them. They were not where they were meant to be, but she couldn't remember where that was. She shut her eyes for a moment to think.

"She's dead!" she heard Blanca scream. "She's dying right here in front of me!" Mimi did not open her eyes to reassure them, or shut Blanca up, but lay in the darkness, riding the pulsing pain.

She heard Miss Lode's voice then, shouting at the children to stand back, but she was drowned out by the boys arguing.

"How could you do that to Mimi?" Casper was yelling. "Look, you've hurt her!"

"Hands off, asshole," Ian retorted. "What makes you the playground police? Besides, you should talk. Rod's black eye is turning green."

"Hey, man, we all saw you pull Mimi down. You're in big trouble now."

"More trouble than you're in? Aren't you suspended? If I recall, suspended students can't be on school property. You're not even supposed to be here. If the teachers see you, they'll expel you. Your ass is grass, amigo, so do us all a favor and get the hell out of here."

Anger. Disdain. Fear. Cunning. With her eyes shut, Mimi's hearing became so heightened that she could monitor every shifting tone in Ian's voice as he tried to move the focus onto Casper. And he was swearing, when he never swore. *Why did I ever go with him?* she thought. *The most mismatched couple ever.*

"Boys! Stop that! Blanca, move aside." Miss Lode was kneeling now and patting Mimi's cheek.

Her eyes blinked open. "She's alive!" Blanca cried.

"Mimi, how do you feel? Does anything hurt?"

"My head hurts, but I can't feel anything else." Mimi tried to move her legs but couldn't tell if she succeeded. She felt frozen.

"Rod, run and tell Mrs. Duke to call an ambulance." Miss Lode kept her voice calm, but Mimi could hear the panic underneath. "Oh, where's Richard? He'd know what to do!"

Rod was staring down at Mimi.

"Quickly, please." Miss Lode raised her voice. "Go! And Blanca, run find Mr. Brabant and tell him to come out here."

Blanca and Rod shook themselves, then ran toward the school entrance.

The flickering aura from earlier was returning to Mimi's vision, and she knew she was heading for the mother of all headaches. She fixed her eyes on Osei, still atop the jungle gym. He looked terrible, his dark skin sporting a surprising gray sheen. She did not know black people could go pale.

King of the jungle, she thought. *But he is a miserable king.*

"Osei," she called up to him, "is this what you were going to show me?" Mimi rolled her head toward the pencil case, though it hurt.

O nodded.

"Mimi, it's best not to speak now," Miss Lode interjected. "Just rest." She raised her voice again. "All of you—time to go home. And Casper, what are you doing here? You're suspended!"

But no one was paying any attention to her.

"How do you think Blanca got that case?" Mimi said.

O frowned. "Casper gave it to her, after Dee gave it to him. She is going with him too. He is a two-timer, just like Dee."

Casper shook his head. "No, man, I don't know what you're talking about. I'm not going with Dee. I never have. And Blanca kept saying that too about the case, and wouldn't listen when I said I didn't give it to her."

Ian was also shaking his head. "Don't," he mouthed at Mimi.

Mimi ignored him. He had already hurt her. What more could he do? "Osei, I bet Blanca got that case from Ian, who told her it was from Casper."

Miss Lode looked from one to the other. "What are you all talking about?" she pleaded.

Osei stared at Mimi. "How do you know?"

"Because I gave the case to Ian. Dee accidentally dropped it and I gave it to him rather than back to her."

"But why? Why did you do that?"

"Do you want to know what Mimi did?" Ian began. "She's a real little bitch."

"Ian! Don't use that language! Stop it, all of you! Oh, where is Richard? Where is Mrs. Duke? I don't know what to do!" Miss Lode was crying now.

"I gave the case to Ian because he wanted it," Mimi said, speaking only to Osei, "and I used it to get him to break up with me. Otherwise I would always be under his power, and I couldn't stand that. I'm sorry," she added. "I didn't know he would use it against you." Though even as she said it, Mimi knew she was dodging the truth. She had understood when she gave it to him that Ian would never have used the pencil case for anything other than evil.

Osei was staring at her. *Can I not trust even you?* his look said.

Mimi blinked away tears, overcome with remorse for playing her part, so against type. She was going to have to live with that.

Now Osei turned his attention to Ian. "Why have you done this thing?"

Ian shrugged. "Because I can."

Miss Lode had been listening to the children as if she'd been given a math problem she couldn't make sense of. "Mimi, whose fault is this?" she whispered.

"Ian," Mimi replied. "It's all Ian."

Miss Lode took a deep breath, wiped her eyes, and got to her feet. "Ian, what do you have to say for yourself?"

"Nothing. I have nothing more to say." Ian pushed his lips tight together, to make clear that he wouldn't say another word. He reminded Mimi of a young boy caught in the act of doing something naughty—a knave, she thought drowsily—and closing his eyes, thinking if he couldn't see anyone, maybe no one could see him. He began to back away, his eyes darting here and there, as if looking for an escape route.

The heavy steps of an adult pounded toward them. "What in God's name is going on here?" Mimi heard Mr. Brabant before she could see him. "Where's Dee?"

"She went home," Casper replied. "I think."

"Is she all right?"

"I guess so."

"What do you mean, you 'guess so'?"

Casper was silent.

When Mr. Brabant's snarling face came into view, it wore the ugliest expression Mimi had ever seen. He hardly looked at her on the ground before turning his fury upward. "Osei, what have you done to Mimi? Come down at once! I warned you!"

His words did not seem to affect O: the new boy remained crouched on top of the jungle gym, gazing impassively at his teacher.

A siren in the distance was gradually getting closer.

"Richard, I don't think—"

"Did you hear me, boy?" Mr. Brabant was incandescent, like a light bulb popping. "Get down from there, nigger!"

Mimi jerked her head—the only part of her that she could move. Her parents had taught her that you never used that word. Never. Ever. You did not even think it.

The rest of the students were still and silent, rigid with the shock of hearing the word aloud—except for Ian, who continued to back away from the scene.

"Stop that!" Miss Lode cried. She had turned bright red. Mimi thought she was telling Ian to stop, but then she continued. "Stop that right now! You do *not* use that language, Richard. You do *not*."

Mr. Brabant showed no sign of hearing her, but was glaring at Osei. The new boy was moving now: not climbing down, but standing up and balancing precariously on the top bars of the jungle gym. Hands free, he swayed above the playground. Then he clenched his hand into a fist and held it high, all the while staring fiercely down at Mr. Brabant. Mimi had seen that gesture before, in a photograph somewhere.

"You know what?" he said, not loud, but penetrating nonetheless. "Black *is* beautiful!"

"Osei, please come down now." Mrs. Duke's calm, authoritative voice emerged from somewhere behind Mimi's head, accompanied by her cloying perfume. "I think we've had enough drama for one day."

Osei glanced at her. "You want me to come down?" he responded, equally calmly.

"Yes, please."

He swung his gaze back to Mr. Brabant. "Do *you* want me to come down?" He said this a little louder.

Though Mr. Brabant continued to glare at Osei, he nodded.

"All right. I will come down now." Fist still raised, O began teetering back and forth. Was it accidental or deliberate? Mimi wasn't sure.

"Stop that!" Mr. Brabant shouted, though he must have understood by now that he was powerless.

Mimi wanted to add: *Don't end up like me.* Because she could not move her legs. This must be her last day ever on this playground. And Ian—Casper had grabbed him by the arms and stopped him from escaping. Ian was sure to be suspended, or worse. And Dee—could she ever come back after all that had been said and done in her name?

There was only Osei left, the king swaying on his throne. He would have to choose. Had chosen, Mimi realized. Just before he plummeted, she heard Miss Lode cry, "Osei, don't!" Then darkness overtook her, and the scene went black.

Hogarth ⓗ *Shakespeare*

He was not of an age, but for all time.
—*Ben Jonson*

For more than four hundred years, Shakespeare's works have been performed, read, and loved throughout the world. They have been reinterpreted for each new generation, whether as teen films, musicals, science-fiction flicks, Japanese warrior tales, or literary transformations. The Hogarth Press was founded by Virginia and Leonard Woolf in 1917 with a mission to publish the best new writing of the age. In 2012, Hogarth was launched in London and New York to continue the tradition. The Hogarth Shakespeare project sees Shakespeare's works retold by acclaimed and bestselling novelists of today.

35674056513782